# Thy Brother Death

## Books by E. X. Ferrars

ANSWER CAME THERE NONE
BEWARE OF THE DOG
DANGER FROM THE DEAD
SLEEP OF THE UNJUST
SMOKE WITHOUT FIRE
WOMAN SLAUGHTER
TRIAL BY FURY
A MURDER TOO MANY
COME TO BE KILLED
THE OTHER DEVIL'S NAME
I MET MURDER
THE CRIME AND THE CRYSTAL
ROOT OF ALL EVIL
SOMETHING WICKED
DEATH OF A MINOR
  CHARACTER
SKELETON IN SEARCH
  OF A CLOSET
THINNER THAN WATER
EXPERIMENT WITH DEATH
FROG IN THE THROAT
DESIGNS ON LIFE
WITNESS BEFORE THE FACT
IN AT THE KILL
MURDERS ANONYMOUS
PRETTY PINK SHROUD
BLOOD FLIES UPWARDS
THE CUP AND THE LIP
ALIVE AND DEAD
HANGED MAN'S HOUSE

THE SMALL WORLD OF MURDER
FOOT IN THE GRAVE
BREATH OF SUSPICION
A STRANGER AND AFRAID
SEVEN SLEEPERS
SKELETON STAFF
THE SWAYING PILLARS
ZERO AT THE BONE
THE DECAYED GENTLEWOMAN
THE DOUBLY DEAD
THE WANDERING WIDOWS
SEEING DOUBLE
SLEEPING DOGS
FEAR THE LIGHT
DEPART THIS LIFE
COUNT THE COST
KILL OR CURE
WE HAVEN'T SEEN HER LATELY
ENOUGH TO KILL A HORSE
ALIBI FOR A WITCH
THE CLOCK THAT WOULDN'T
  STOP
HUNT THE TORTOISE
THE MARCH MURDERS
CHEAT THE HANGMAN
I, SAID THE FLY
NECK IN A NOOSE
THE SHAPE OF A STAIN
MURDER OF A SUICIDE
REHEARSALS FOR A MURDER

# Thy Brother Death

## E. X. FERRARS

A PERFECT CRIME BOOK
DOUBLEDAY
New York   London   Toronto   Sydney   Auckland

A PERFECT CRIME BOOK
PUBLISHED BY DOUBLEDAY
a division of Bantam Doubleday Dell Publishing Group, Inc.
1540 Broadway, New York, New York 10036

DOUBLEDAY is a trademark of Doubleday,
a division of Bantam Doubleday Dell Publishing Group, Inc.

Library of Congress Cataloging-in-Publication Data

Ferrars, E. X.
Thy brother death/E. X. Ferrars.—1st ed. in the U.S.A.
p.  cm.
"A Perfect crime book."
1. College teachers—England—Fiction. 2. Brothers—England—
Fiction. I. Title.
PR6003.R458T55   1993
823'.912—dc20   93-23187
CIP

ISBN 0-385-47092-4
Copyright © 1993 by M. D. Brown
All Rights Reserved
Printed in the United States of America
November 1993
First Edition in the United States of America

1  3  5  7  9  10  8  6  4  2

# Thy Brother Death

# One

The ringing of the telephone in the next room woke Henrietta Carey from the doze that she had drifted into after lunch and it was bringing her to her feet when she remembered where she was. She was staying with her mother. It was most unlikely that the call would be for her. She sank back into the chair where she had been reading a detective story, found the book was on the floor at her feet, picked it up and started looking for the place that she had reached when it had helped to put her to sleep.

Henrietta was forty. She was a small woman, neatly made, with hair that had gone grey early and was cropped short and an oval face that had stayed young for her age. Her eyes, when she was fully awake, were bright and dark, with long, dark lashes, her nose was short and turned up a little, her mouth was wide and smiled easily, showing fine white teeth. She was wearing black slacks and a white sweater that had been knitted for her by her mother, who had very little else to do these days but knit. Henrietta visited her mother about twice a year and always found it very restful.

But after a moment her mother put her head into the room.

'It's for you,' she said.

'Patrick?' Henrietta asked.

'Yes,' her mother answered, 'and he sounds in a bit of a state, though when I asked him if anything was the matter he said, oh dear no, nothing at all, and he asked me how I was, and so on. But if I were you I'd be prepared for hearing that he's had a smash in the car or lost his job.'

'He can't lose his job,' Henrietta said. 'It's permanent. He's got tenure. They can't get rid of him till he's sixty-five.'

Patrick Carey, who was Henrietta's husband, was a senior lecturer in the Biochemistry Department of the University of Knotlington. She was not as alarmed as she might have been by what her mother had said because it was not unusual, when she was away from home, for Patrick to telephone, sounding as if some accident of considerable seriousness had just happened to him. On the other hand, on an occasion when a real accident had happened, he had been calmness itself.

On that occasion he had opened the conversation by telling her that there was nothing to worry about, that he was perfectly all right and that she need not dream of hurrying home. This was all before he had told her what had happened, which was that he had unfortunately forgotten his door-key and locked himself out of their flat, had endeavoured to re-enter it by climbing up a drainpipe to the bathroom window which happened to be open, had almost reached it when he had slipped and fallen on to the concrete path below, and that the only damage that he had done to himself was to break a bone in his heel. A mere nothing, but Henrietta had been on the next train back to Knotlington.

Their doctor had told her then that he had been lucky not to break his back, for the house in which they lived, which had been converted into flats, was Victorian, with high ceilings, and the fall from near the bathroom window, on the middle floor of the house, had been a long one. So the fact that today Patrick was in a state instead of being very calm suggested to Henrietta that at worst he had some bitter complaint to make about the behaviour of his professor, Margaret Franks, for whom, unfortunately he had lately formed a ferocious dislike, after two or three years of ardently admiring her.

Going into the next door room and picking up the telephone, Henrietta said, 'It's me.'

'Henrietta, a very strange thing has happened,' Patrick

said. She could hear the effort he had to make to keep his voice level. 'I don't know if it means anything or not.'

'What is it?' she asked.

'I found a letter on my desk this morning,' he said, 'addressed to Professor Carey. Just Professor Carey, Knotlington University, Knotlington. It had been opened, of course, by Professor Carey himself, but he'd said, so Julie Bishop told me, that it was nothing to do with him and suggested it might be meant for me, as my name was Carey too, so it had been put in my room.'

Julie Bishop was Professor Margaret Franks's secretary, and Professor Eustace Carey was Professor of Psychology in the University.

'But you're not a professor,' Henrietta said.

'No, but I'm the only other Carey in the place and Eustace swears it's nothing to do with him.'

'Well, what was in the letter?' Henrietta asked.

'It was from a woman in Aberdeen, demanding maintenance from Professor Carey, since he was her husband, and threatening to take court action if the money wasn't forthcoming. It was just signed E.'

Henrietta began to laugh. 'So dear old Eustace is a bigamist! A wife in Knotlington, and another in Aberdeen! That's certainly surprising, but I don't see why you should worry about it.'

'I'm not worried. Of course I'm not worried. Not exactly. I gave the letter, which naturally has been read by everyone in the department by now, to Julie and said it was nothing to do with me. And I don't know what she's done with it, and I didn't think anything more about it, and then suddenly—it was just before lunch—I had a rather fearful thought. Could it be anything to do with David, I wondered. Has he been up to something?'

'Oh,' Henrietta said. 'Oh, I see.'

'D'you think that's likely?'

'Likely? I don't know. I suppose it isn't impossible.' Her tone had become thoughtful.

'You do think it might be David's doing, don't you?' He had heard the change in her voice.

'But even if it is, Patrick, it's got nothing to do with you. You aren't responsible for him.'

'But what ought I to do about it?'

'Nothing.'

'Nothing at all?'

'No, how can you do anything?'

'Oh, I don't know, it's just that I feel . . . Well, you know how I feel about him.'

'Yes, but you don't even know that this letter has anything to do with him.'

'You believe it was really meant for Eustace?'

'It doesn't seem probable, I admit, but he's a professor and you aren't.'

'So you'd really do nothing about it.'

'Yes.'

He took a moment to think it over, then said uncertainly, 'I suppose you're right. Only, if it is David . . .'

'You know you can't do anything about him. He's incurable.'

'I suppose so. Yes. I'm sure you're right. Do nothing, and hope we hear nothing more about it.'

'I'd say that's the only thing to do. How's everything else? Are you all right?'

'Oh yes, fine, fine. I could murder the Franks bitch for what she did this morning, but that's just by the way. How are you?'

'Wonderfully rested. We went to the theatre yesterday. *Uncle Vanya*. I think it's about the third time I've seen it.'

'I wouldn't mind seeing it a fourth. When are you coming home?'

'As I told you, on Friday.'

'It's just that we're giving a party on Saturday. I hope that's all right.'

'You mean the department's giving a party?'

'No, no, you and me. At home. A very small party. Only about half a dozen people.'

'Is there some special reason for it?'

'Only that we've a visiting American on our hands and I think he may have been finding things a bit dismal. Margaret hasn't exactly put herself out to welcome him, so I thought we might do something.'

'Well, if you'll organize everything, I mean, get in the drinks and so on, I suppose it's all right. I shan't have much time to do any of it, getting home only on Friday afternoon.'

'Oh yes. I can do that. And you don't think I ought to do anything about that letter from Aberdeen?'

'I'd at least wait and see if anything more happens. But do what you think best yourself, Patrick.'

'I think I'll do nothing. Give my love to your mother. I'm missing you, Henrietta. I'm looking forward to Friday.'

'So am I, strange as it may seem.'

'Goodbye.'

'Goodbye.'

They both rang off.

For a moment Henrietta stayed where she was, staring down at the telephone, as if in itself it posed a puzzling problem, then, frowning a little, she wandered back into the next door room and dropped down in the chair where she had been sitting when the telephone rang.

Her mother was now sitting on the sofa under the window, busy knitting. Mrs Lanchester, who was sixty-five and who had been matron of a small private hospital until her retirement at sixty, was a squarely built, somewhat plump woman, with dark hair not as grey as her daughter's, a square, pink face, grey eyes and a smile that could look curiously stern. She was accustomed to authority, though

Henrietta had long ago learnt the knack of resisting it when she chose. Her mother gave her a thoughtful look as she came in.

'You look worried,' she said.

Henrietta did not reply at once, then she told her mother most of what Patrick had said in his call. Repeating it, it sounded even more absurd than it had when Patrick had told her about the letter.

Mrs Lanchester burst out laughing.

'If the first thing Patrick does when he's accused of bigamy is to consult you, you've nothing to worry about,' she said.

'It isn't that that's worrying me.'

'I realize that. It's David, isn't it?'

Henrietta nodded, her frown deepening.

Mrs Lanchester had let her knitting sink into her lap, but picking it up, she went to work again.

'You'll have to stop worrying about him, won't you?' she said. 'You can't let him make a complete mess of your lives.'

'That's more or less what I told Patrick,' Henrietta said, 'but this time we really don't know what he may have been up to. If whatever's happened is actually his doing at all. It's only a nasty feeling we've both got that perhaps it is. Anything peculiar that happens to us these days we tend to put down to him, unless Patrick gets it into his head it's the doing of Margaret Franks.'

'It's a pity he and she have got across each other so badly.'

'Yes, but I honestly don't think it's Patrick fault. She's a very difficult woman. Brilliant, of course, an FRS and all that, but something human got left out of her at her birth.'

'But she can't have anything to do with this letter from Aberdeen.'

'No, I didn't mean that. No, if that's actually got anything to do with us, then David's responsible.'

David Carey was Patrick's brother, five years the younger. Both of them had been born in Kenya, where their father, a fierce, stubborn man, had been a farmer, staying there with bitter determination through the Mau Mau days and on into the days of independence. Their mother had died when David was ten, and neither of the boys had had much experience of tenderness or even kindness at their father's hands, though in his fashion he had probably loved them both. It was a fashion, however, bullying and aggressive, that had led Patrick to escape from him as soon as he could to London University, and from the time that he had achieved that, he had never been back to his home.

David, on the other hand, had developed a different method of dealing with his father's rages, heavy drinking and occasional outbursts of sentimental affection. He always yielded to them, always conciliated him, and if the easiest way to do this had been to tell a few lies, he had told them without hesitation. In fact, he had become an accomplished and imaginative liar, by degrees learning actually to prefer falsehood to truth.

He had stayed with his father until he was over thirty, when the old man had died, leaving the farm and all that he had to David. This relative wealth had not lasted long. After two years, David had arrived in England, nearly penniless, and at once had picked up the relationship with Patrick, who by then was a senior lecturer in Knotlington. When David's first letter reached him he had been delighted. Though nothing would have taken him back to Kenya, there had always been a sore spot in his heart because of the complete break with his family. David had written that he had acquired an excellent job with a big firm of caterers in London and was making good money, and that he would like to come to Knotlington to spend a weekend with Patrick and Henrietta. He was warmly invited to come. And within ten minutes of being in their flat he had managed to extract fifty pounds from Patrick, who unfortunately had been to the bank that morning and it had soon turned out that the firm of caterers did not exist. And that had been only the beginning.

How David had managed to subsist since then Patrick and Henrietta had never been sure, but they had been certain that it had not been by working in any of the fine jobs he had always claimed that he was in when he came to visit them. They became cautious about lending him money and about believing anything that he told them of himself. He had a curious way, they had learnt, of intently listening to what someone might disclose of himself, and when next he had a chance of talking of himself, he would become that person, whether he was a civil servant, a parson, an engineer, or perhaps a policeman. Patrick had wondered how often David had passed himself off to unsuspecting people as a senior lecturer in a midland university. Yet a kind of affection had survived between the brothers. Patrick had made several efforts to persuade David that there was no special virtue in dishonesty, that lies seldom paid much better than the truth, and that it would really be in his interest to go to a psychiatrist. Seriously challenged about his world of fantasy, David was liable to dissolve in tears, claim that he could not help what he did, would certainly go to a psychiatrist and do anything else that Patrick suggested that would help him to become a worthy citizen. But when Patrick had discovered a psychiatrist who was ready to take David on at a price that Patrick had thought he could afford, it would turn out that David had changed his lodgings, leaving no address behind, and no more would be heard of him till one day he would telephone and suggest that he should visit Knotlington.

After a few tries Patrick had given up any attempt to reform his brother. By what means he had managed to live, unless it was simply on unemployment benefit, Patrick had never discovered. Crime of some sort did not seem impossible, but if that was how David managed, Patrick preferred not to know about it.

However, when a letter came from Aberdeen to a Professor Carey at Knotlington University, claiming that he had married a woman there, was failing to support her and had apparently deserted her, and since Professor Eustace Carey, a man near retirement, with a wife and three grown-up children, had said that the letter had nothing to do with him and someone had had the bright idea of handing it on to Patrick, as if it was not inconceivable that he might be a bigamist, it was not altogether surprising that his thoughts should have gone at once to David.

But where, Henrietta wondered as she sat absent-mindedly watching her mother calmly and rhythmically knitting, was David now? And could the preposterous letter involve Patrick in trouble?

While her knitting-needles flashed, Mrs Lanchester's eyes were on Henrietta's face.

'I really shouldn't worry too much,' she said. 'Even if it's David's doing, whatever it is, it's nothing to do with you.'

'But it's such a strange thing to have done,' Henrietta said, 'marrying someone in Patrick's name—because that's what it sounds as if he's done, doesn't it?'

'I wouldn't put it past him,' her mother said. She had met David a few times and through her medical contacts had been the person who had found a psychiatrist for him. 'We've only got to hope it's nothing worse than that.'

'What could be worse, in the circumstances?'

'Oh, murder, blackmail, arson, kidnapping, grievous bodily harm.'

'But none of those fit that letter.'

'No, dear, I was just trying to cheer you up. That letter isn't the end of the world.'

'No,' Henrietta said, 'but I can't help feeling it's the beginning of something.'

*

On Friday morning Henrietta packed her suitcase, said goodbye to her mother and took a taxi to Euston. She had lunch on the train and arrived in Knotlington at about half past two. She was used to that arrival by now, the invariable pause that the train made by the great gas cylinders on the edge of the town, the view of roofs and chimneys, the sense of human beings packed more densely together than could ever possibly seem right and the general greyness of everything, but she never quite forgot the dismay that she had felt when she had seen it for the first time.

That was three years ago. She and Patrick had come from a pleasant green village in Berkshire, near to Reading, where he had been a lecturer, and although the move to Knotlington and the appointment as a senior lecturer there had been promotion, it had also been Henrietta's first experience of an industrial town in the Midlands. And even now, when she had developed quite an affection for the place, some of that dismay still made itself felt whenever she returned to it, even if the fact was that it was not nearly as crowded, as noisy or as dirty as London, which she had always loved.

She did not expect Patrick to be at the station to meet her, as on a Friday afternoon she knew that he would be taking a practical class. She took another taxi, gave their address and reached their home in about a quarter of an hour. It was at the top of a steep road which at the time when it had been built up had been the beginning of the suburbs, almost countrified. All the old houses along it were large, with big gardens, but a good many of these had bungalows wedged in between the original buildings, most of which, like the one in which the Careys lived, had been converted into flats. It was the property of the University and the Careys had been able to rent their flat instead of having to take out a mortgage to buy a house of their own. That they had never seriously thought of doing this in one of the more charming villages in the hills outside the

town was a sign, Henrietta thought, that Patrick did not
feel as secure or contented in his job as he usually made
out.

That, of course, was because of Margaret Franks, though
it had been she who had persuaded him to come to Knotlington and who had promised him great advantages in his
work, splendid facilities, as well as the attraction of her
warm friendship. It had been very warm. Too warm not
to be dangerous. What fools they had been, Henrietta had
often reflected in more recent times, not to foresee that.
The only person to foresee it and to utter one or two warn-
ings had been Mrs Lanchester, but though she had dropped
a few sardonic remarks on the situation, she would not
have dreamt of interfering. It had always been almost an
impossibility to induce her to offer advice on anything and
in any case no one, even people who were eager to do
so, had ever found it profitable to try to advise Patrick.
The house in the Berkshire village had been sold for
a very satisfactory sum, for the slump in the housing
market had not yet begun, and the Careys had moved to
Knotlington.

Their flat was a pleasant one, occupying the middle floor
of a square red brick building. Its rooms were spacious,
with tall windows and high ceilings, and it had had enough
modernization done to it to make it comfortable. The central heating was adequate, the bathroom was new and
bright, the kitchen, which was large and served at one end
as a pleasant dining-room, had a dishwasher, refrigerator,
freezer and plenty of cupboards in a reasonable plastic ver-
sion of teak. The bow window in the sitting-room over-
looked a wide lawn and a shrubbery which had not yet
suffered the fate of being carved up to accommodate
bungalows.

The Careys' neighbours were also members of the University. In the flat below them lived a Dr Charles Hedden, a
bachelor of about Patrick's age, whose flat was considerably

larger than theirs, but who lived mostly in one room of it, surrounded by a wild disorder of books, papers, computers, word-processors, tape-recorders, clothes that were not put away in the ample cupboards provided for them, and who was a reader in the Department of Mediæval History.

In the top flat, which was the smallest in the house, lived a young couple who had recently acquired a baby. Their name was Quinn. Simon Quinn was in a temporary research unit in the Department of Biochemistry, to which he had been introduced by Patrick in the days when Margaret Franks was still ready to do anything that Patrick suggested. Patrick had encountered him at a scientific conference in Glasgow, had learnt that the grant on which he had subsisted in London for the last two years was just coming to an end, and since in conversation he had been impressed by the young man's ability, had managed to find room for him in the research unit which he directed himself in Knotlington. Simon Quinn had arrived with a new wife, and now they had added a baby to the family. It was a child that cried a good deal, and neither of the Quinns seemed particularly well qualified to cope with it, but luckily the walls of the house were thick and the floors solid, so the noise was not too disturbing. The Careys regarded themselves as fortunate in their neighbours.

Henrietta unpacked her suitcase, then went prowling round the flat to see what condition it had got into during her brief absence. It was clean and tidy enough, since Mrs Forbes, their help, would have come in as usual on Monday and Thursday, to vacuum, polish and scrub and though Patrick, scientist that he might be, had never learnt how to use the dishwasher, he was conscientious about rinsing the crockery that he had used under the hot tap, so there was no accumulation of dishes and glasses that needed attention. But was there anything for them to eat that evening, Henrietta wondered, or would they have to go out?

She was tired and wanted to stay at home and was glad

to find some moussaka in the freezer, as well as a rather mysterious bread and butter pudding in the fridge. The pudding puzzled her. It was unthinkable that Patrick should have made it himself, yet it had a homemade look about it and certainly had not come out of a packet. The answer, almost certainly, was that it was a present from Rachel Quinn. Whenever she had been baking, she was always generous to the Careys and to Charles Hedden with presents of cakes, and she would have thought it natural, when Henrietta was away, to see that Patrick did not lack for puddings. So all that Henrietta would have to do that evening was warm up the pudding and the moussaka.

Meanwhile she made herself some tea and carried it into the sitting-room, where she lit the gas fire, for though the central heating was reasonably efficient, the February afternoon had a clammy chill. There were raindrops on the window-panes, not by any means a downpour, but enough to fill the air with dampness. The leafless trees in the garden looked gaunt and somehow lonely. But there were some African violets in a pot on a table in the bow window, a sign that Patrick had been thinking of her homecoming. The sight of them gave her a little glow of pleasure. Sitting down by the fire, she drank her tea, then leant back and incautiously closed her eyes. When Patrick came in at about six o'clock she was still there, fast asleep.

He woke her by hauling her to her feet and kissing her and when she had come to herself she kissed him back, told him that the African violets were lovely and that it would be nice now to have some sherry.

It was dark outside the window. Its wide sheets of plate glass only reflected the room and Patrick and Henrietta in it. He crossed to the window and drew the curtains. He was a tall, lean man with thick fair hair above a narrow face, somewhat bony features, a sharp beak of a nose and wide-spaced grey eyes, the expression of which was usually singularly mild but which were capable, without warning, of becoming brilliant with the flare of a remarkable anger. Henrietta suspected that this was something that he had inherited from his father, though he would have fiercely denied that he had inherited anything from that ferocious man.

He was wearing twill slacks, a dark blue shirt and a tweed jacket, which he removed when he had finished kissing Henrietta again and replaced it with a red and grey cardigan which had been knitted for him several years ago by Mrs Lanchester and from which he would not be parted. Then he fetched the sherry and glasses from the kitchen, poured out the sherry, sat down and said, 'Well, as to what we were talking about, I did as you said. I did nothing at all. Nothing. And now look what's happened.'

'About that letter, do you mean?' Henrietta asked.

He nodded earnestly.

'Well, what has happened?' she asked.

'Another letter,' he said. 'And this time the bloody thing is correctly addressed.'

'Actually to you?'

'Yes, to Dr Patrick Carey, 2 Curlingham House, Tenterfield Road, Knotlington.'

'You mean it came to you here, not to the University?'

'Yes.'

'When?'

'This morning.'

'And it's just signed E., like the other one?'

He nodded again.

'And it's from someone who thinks she's your wife?' she asked.

'So it seems.'

'Perhaps I ought to see it,' Henrietta suggested.

He had it ready in his hand, to show her. On the envelope, typewritten, was his address, as he had said, Dr Patrick Carey, 2 Curlingham House, Tenterfield Road, Knotlington. Inside it was a brief letter, also typewritten, with an address at the top, 12 Birdway Gardens, Aberdeen. The letter said:

> Dear Pat, Not that you are very dear to me at the moment. Are you going to send me that money you promised me, and to which I am entitled as your wife? Perhaps my last letter to you went astray, but I assure you that I mean to do as I said in it, I shall get a lawyer on to the job and he will take you to court. Haven't I done everything I agreed to and been very patient with you? But you can't expect that to last for ever. E.

Henrietta read the letter twice, then refolded it, put it into the envelope and handed it back to Patrick.

After a moment she said, 'It must be David's doing.'

'You mean he's married someone in my name?' Patrick asked.

'Isn't that what it's got to mean?'

'It's going a bit far, even for him, isn't it?'

'Oh, I don't know about that. We don't really know how he's been keeping going this last year or so. He must have had some source of income. For all we know he's got several wives.'

'So you think he married this unfortunate woman simply to be able to live on her?'

'And then found she expected to live on him so he removed himself? She seems to have thought he was a professor, after all. That seems to explain things, more or less.'

'But what does she mean by saying she's done everything she'd agreed to do? Somehow I don't like the sound of it.'

'You think she may have been his accomplice in something?'

'Well, I expect there are dishonest people in Aberdeen, as well as everywhere else.'

'But he hasn't kept his side of their agreement, whatever that was, and she means to get even with him?'

'That's how it looks, doesn't it?'

He stood up and put the letter down on the mantelpiece.

'There's one thing we could try,' he said, 'and I almost did, the other evening, but then I followed your advice and did nothing.'

'Yes?' she said.

'We've her address, so we could see if she's got a telephone. I could ring Directory Enquiries and see if we can get through to her.'

'Do we really want to get through to her?' Henrietta asked.

'Why shouldn't we?'

'I'm not sure what good it would do. You and David have voices that sound very much alike. If you rang her up and simply told her that you weren't the man who'd married her, she'd be quite likely not to believe you.'

'Who would she think I was, then?'

'Well, I don't suppose he's mentioned that he's got a brother. If you said that's who you were, she'd naturally think it was a trick. He's fairly obviously deserted her. I'd really be inclined to do nothing and just to wait and see what happens.'

'You think something *will* happen?'

'It doesn't seem altogether unlikely. Of course, if it does and leads to trouble, you might take the two letters to Pym and Gerbold.'

Pym and Gerbold were the Careys' lawyers in London who handled their modest investments for them. They were also the Carey family lawyers, who had looked after the remaining interests in England of Patrick's and David's father, and who knew a certain amount about David's character, and how the money that the sale of the farm in Kenya had brought had managed to vanish in two years.

Patrick nodded. 'Yes, if there's trouble with this woman. I suppose we could do that.'

'Meanwhile, what about this party we're supposed to be

giving tomorrow?' Henrietta asked. 'And what had Margaret done the other morning that made you think you'd like to murder her?'

He had so often wanted to murder her lately that Henrietta, till then, had not given that matter much thought.

'Oh, it was about the American,' Patrick answered. 'Heinzman. He's from Berkeley, and he's over here for two or three months. He came to Knotlington partly to see me, though there were one or two other people he wanted to see too. He and I have been working along related lines for the last few years, and it seemed a good opportunity to have some discussion about it. He came to see me on Monday, and we spent most of the day together. Very interesting chap, very rewarding. But then he turned up again for some more of the same next day and happened to run into Margaret on the stairs. And she told him that we were a very busy department and that I ought to be getting on with my own work instead of gossiping with him, and virtually turned him out. I happened to come along at the end of her outburst and went off with him, but naturally I had a good deal of difficulty in calming him down after her rudeness. So that's when I thought of asking a few people, to show him we aren't all savages.'

'And he's coming to it?'

'Oh yes.'

'And who else?'

'Some of the department, and Charlie, of course, and Simon and Rachel.' By Charlie he meant Charles Hedden, who lived in the flat below, and Simon and Rachel were the Quinns, who lived in the flat above.

'You don't mean you've asked Margaret,' Henrietta said.

'Oh, I asked her,' Patrick said. 'I didn't want to give her an additional grievance by leaving her out. And she mumbled something, but of course she won't come. I hope not, anyway.'

'What made her turn on the poor fellow like that?'

'God knows. Jealousy, perhaps, that he'd come to see me and Robarts and not her.'

Neil Robarts was another senior lecturer in the Department of Biochemistry.

'She is jealous of you, I suppose.' Henrietta might have added that it was in more ways than one. Margaret Franks was probably jealous of the fact that scientifically Patrick had been making his mark without having to depend on her as much as she had expected when she appointed him, but also there was another kind of jealousy which was more destructive, jealousy that Henrietta felt was directed mainly against herself. For Margaret Franks to be satisfied, Henrietta should not have existed. It was the fact that she did, Henrietta believed, that made Margaret as bitter and aggressive as she often was.

'You've got in all we need for the party, have you?' she said.

'I think we've got enough of everything,' Patrick answered. 'Just wine and some smoked salmon and olives and pâté and that sort of thing. If there's anything more you think we ought to have, I'll get it tomorrow.'

'And for supper tonight we're having moussaka and bread and butter pudding, are we?'

'If that's all right.'

'I suppose Rachel brought you the pudding.'

'Yes. She and Simon have looked after me splendidly while you've been away. I've eaten with them most evenings, and they asked the two of us up there this evening as well, only I said I thought you'd be tired and would probably sooner stay at home.'

'Quite right.' She looked round the room, the furnishings of which she and Patrick had acquired bit by bit as they had moved from place to place during the fifteen years of their marriage. There was a Georgian tallboy, an older carved chest, some chairs that might be Hepplewhite but probably were not, a modern coffee table, a small round

Victorian table in the window on which Patrick had put the African violets, some comfortable and rather shabby easy chairs, a wall covered with books and a television on a stand in one corner. A muddle of a room, but one in which almost each item had some meaning for both her and Patrick.

'It's good to be back, even if we've got a few odd things to worry about,' she said.

'D'you know what's really worrying me?' Patrick said, and his narrow, expressive face was suddenly sombre. 'The letter I got this morning was correctly addressed, wasn't it?'

'Yes,' she agreed.

'And the one that was dumped on me in the department wasn't. It was simply addressed to a Professor Carey, Knotlington University, who perhaps doesn't even exist.'

'So you said.'

'So between the time that that got to me and this morning, the woman E., whoever she is, had been sent a note of my correct title and my home address.'

'Yes.'

'Well, who in the department hates me enough to have done that? That first letter went the round of the place. Everyone saw it. And one of them seems to believe I'm a bigamist and has gone to the trouble to try to stir up trouble for me. Well, you know them all. Take your pick. Which of them did that?'

# *Two*

Henrietta went out to the kitchen, lit the oven and put the moussaka and the bread and butter pudding into it, then she returned to the sitting-room and poured out some more sherry for herself.

'Does it have to be someone who hates you?' she said as she settled herself once more in the chair by the fire. 'Mightn't it just be a trick, someone having a bit of fun at your expense?'

'Rather malicious fun, wouldn't you say?' Patrick said.

'Well, yes, whatever way one looks at it, someone at the very least wants to make you look a fool. But hatred . . .' There was something about the idea of hatred that she found frightening. She did not want to believe in it, especially since it would have to be the hatred of someone she and Patrick knew and perhaps even liked.

'Someone who may be coming to our party tomorrow,' Patrick said.

'Did no one outside the department see that first letter?' she asked.

'Oh yes, several people may have seen it. Old Eustace, for instance, as it went first to him as the only real Professor Carey. And we don't know how many other people in his department. But I can't believe he himself would do such a thing as write to E. to give her my proper address, and I don't really know any of his people well enough to think any of them would bother to do a thing like that.'

'So who do you think did it?'

He said nothing, but sat frowning at the glass in his hand.

'Haven't you at least some suspicion?' she asked.

He gave a sigh. 'That's what I've been asking myself all

day, ever since this damned thing came. I somehow took for granted at first it must be Margaret, but honestly I can't see her doing anything so petty. She might shout at me that I'd got to prove that first letter hadn't been meant for me, and make a hell of a row which everyone could hear about my obviously being a bigamist, but I can't see her writing off secretly to that woman in Aberdeen, without saying anything about it to me, just to give her my address. Whatever I may have against Margaret, it's never been that there's anything underhand about her.'

Henrietta agreed with him. Margaret Franks was a woman of violent feelings, but they were all out in the open. That she herself often did not understand them did not mean that they were concealed. Henrietta had always believed that Margaret herself had not understood how much she had been in love with Patrick when she had persuaded him to come to Knotlington. If she had understood her feeling for him she would probably never have dreamt of urging him to come. She would have had some foreknowledge of the pain in store for herself if he did.

And to Patrick, who was singularly unaware of his charm, the possibility that he meant far more to her than was shown in their open friendship had simply not occurred. He had admired her scientific brilliance deeply, had recognized how generous and warm-hearted she could be, and had innocently welcomed her interest in him. But even if she was a remarkably handsome woman who was unmarried and known to have had several lovers and not to be much given to sexless friendships, she was ten years older than he was, and knew that he had a wife to whom he had always made it plain that he was very happily married.

But in the past he and Margaret had usually met at scientific conferences in different parts of the world, in Paris, in Copenhagen, in California, in Sydney, and Henrietta had never been present. She believed that she had never had much reality for Margaret until she had arrived in Knotlington with Patrick. Even then, at first, Margaret had treated her with cheerful friendliness. She had not thought of her as important and it had only been as she had gradually realized that her relationship with Patrick was not developing in intimacy but if anything growing more impersonal, more purely professional, that her own strong feelings for him had begun to change to an increasing bitterness. Yet Henrietta had never managed to dislike her and she agreed with Patrick that it would have been out of character for Margaret to write on the quiet to the woman who claimed to be married to Patrick, to bring ruin on his head.

'All right, we'll agree it can't have been Margaret,' Henrietta said. 'Who's next?'

'There's Julie Bishop, of course,' he answered.

Julie Bishop was Margaret's secretary, a small, plump woman of thirty-three, with a little round face and small, soft-looking features and a pair of singularly steely blue eyes with which she gave the impression of taking in and recording in her memory whatever she observed. She had a mop of auburn curls and very white teeth. She was a native of Knotlington and lived with her parents in the town. She was exceedingly efficient and appeared to feel the deepest admiration for Margaret Franks.

'Yes, she's a possibility,' Henrietta said. 'For one thing, it would come to her naturally to write a letter, particularly if it gave her a chance of putting right such a mistake as addressing you as Professor. We'll keep Julie in mind. Who else?'

'What about Robarts?'

Neil Robarts, a senior lecturer like Patrick, was forty-two, a short, square man, with dark hair already going thin, a heavy, pallid face, dark eyes and thick dark eyebrows that seemed almost to overhang the gold-rimmed spectacles that he wore. He was a very reserved man, almost secretive, with a shy, frightened-looking wife who appeared in the

University as little as she was able. Except for one another, they seemed to have no friends. But he was professionally ambitious, and fairly gifted. Margaret Franks had a way of trying to play him and Patrick off against one another, giving one or other of them her enthusiastic support, though from day to day neither of them knew which it would be. He was one of the people whom hardly anyone ever called by his first name. He was Robarts, not Neil, to nearly everybody.

'I suppose he's a possibility,' Henrietta said, 'but do you think he'd ever come out of his shell enough to bother about what you'd been up to?'

'Perhaps not, though it's difficult to guess what's really going on in his head,' Patrick replied. 'I've never felt sure if he likes or dislikes me.'

'It might be neither. I never feel sure that he's really sure that other people exist. He's coming tomorrow, is he?'

'Yes, and bringing that odd woman he's married to. I didn't really expect him to come, but I think he wants to be on good terms with Heinzman. I've a feeling he's got a daydream of going off to some splendid sort of job in America.'

'Then there's Malcolm Mackintosh,' Henrietta said.

'Ah yes, now that's really a possibility. A Scot who thinks I've been playing fast and loose with a countrywoman of his.'

'Except that Malcolm's the kind of Scot who's spent nearly the whole of his life before coming to Knotlington in the year one in London and probably wouldn't be able to find his way around Edinburgh or Glasgow if he was stranded there. However, I agree we shouldn't cross him off our list. Only he's so near retirement it seems unlikely he'd care about what's going on in the department.'

'That might be why he's a good suspect. He's really got so few other interests left.'

'But he's always so friendly. And talking of friends, we mustn't forget Simon.'

'No, of course not. But even if he were base enough to forget everything I've done for him, it would hardly be in his interest to get me into trouble. His job here is only temporary. Margaret could get rid of him quite easily if she chose.'

'Still, we'll include him.'

They included two or three other people before they grew tired of what they knew was a pointless occupation and settled down to eat their moussaka and pudding. The more they talked about it, the more impossible it seemed that they could possibly guess who it was who either believed that Patrick had committed bigamy in Aberdeen, or who, without in the least believing it, thought that it would be entertaining to involve him in a scandal by sending the unknown woman there his correct title and address.

'Of course, it's possible that whoever it is thinks that I'm the wife you've married bigamously,' Henrietta said. 'E. doesn't say anything about the date of her marriage to you.'

'And I've managed to keep two wives going for fifteen years!' Patrick laughed. 'Be realistic.'

'I suppose it would have been a bit difficult on your salary. But then I used to be earning a bit too. That would have helped.' Before coming to Knotlington Henrietta had worked as a librarian in Reading, but she had not looked for work since their move to the Midlands. 'Even so, I suppose if you'd been married to her for as long as that, she'd have tried to get money out of you, or at least divorced you, before now.'

The seriousness with which they had begun their discussion had evaporated, which she found a relief. From the first she had not been inclined to feel nearly as worried about the matter as Patrick had. But that was only natural. The people whom they had been discussing were not her colleagues. She did not have to come face to face with them day after day. That the source of the trouble, whatever it really was, was Patrick's brother David was certain and if somehow a scandal of dangerous proportions were to blow up, that could always be proved.

She wondered where David was at present and how he was making a living. Probably he was in London, she thought, though it was not altogether impossible that by now he had found his way into prison. But she did not suggest this to Patrick, who had relaxed and grown cheerful and wanted to make love to her. All the same, it might explain why supplies to the woman in Aberdeen appeared to have been fairly recently cut off. If it was not recently that this had happened, she would surely have started making trouble about it sooner. But Henrietta also felt more like making love than going on puzzling about David, about the strange woman E., or even about Margaret Franks, who was the one of the three whom she was inclined to take most seriously.

Next morning Patrick set off as usual to his laboratory, and Henrietta to the supermarket just beyond the corner where Tenterfield Road turned into the main road that led from the centre of the town to the point where it joined the motorway that eventually led to London. Tenterfield Road was quiet, a cul-de-sac that ended at Curlingham House, but the main road was always choked with traffic, some of it moving, and a good deal too fast, some of it stationary, almost blocking it, in spite of double yellow lines beside the pavements. Henrietta did the shopping that she wanted to do for the weekend, and when she had unpacked it on reaching home, went upstairs to the flat above, taking with her the dish that had contained the bread and butter pudding.

Rachel Quinn opened the door when she rang. Rachel was a tall, slim young woman of twenty-three, with a cloud of pale hair which always looked to Henrietta as if she never brushed it, but which quite likely had been carefully arranged to look like that by a local hairdresser. She had large, gentle blue eyes in a delicately pointed face with thin features and a small, fine-lipped mouth. Her slimness was of the kind that looks very fragile, and she often gave the impression of wondering where she was and what she ought to be doing, though Henrietta knew her to be a hardworking, efficient housewife, if not the most practical of mothers. When she had her baby on her knee and was playing with it, as she often did, it looked as if she wondered how it had got there. She was wearing jeans and a man's shirt hanging loose outside them. It was pale blue and probably belonged to Simon.

'I just came up to thank you for helping to look after Patrick while I've been away, and to return this,' Henrietta said, holding out the dish that she had brought. 'It was very good of you.'

'Oh, but you know how we love doing it,' Rachel said. 'Come in.'

She turned and led the way into the living-room in the flat. It was a good deal smaller than the Careys', and with a much lower ceiling. It had two not very large dormer windows and a small fireplace of black iron that had a gas fire set in it. Once the room would have been inhabited by servants. The furniture was all modern, fairly battered second-hand, but cheerful. The fire was alight and had a low fire-guard round it, with various oddments of a child's clothing draped on it today. The baby, now three months old, was on the hearthrug.

'Would you like some coffee?' Rachel asked. 'I was just making some.'

She hardly waited for Henrietta to reply, but disappeared into the kitchen, returning after a minute or two with blue and white striped mugs of instant coffee.

'You don't take sugar, isn't that right?' she said.

Henrietta had sat down in a chair by the fire and was leaning forward, exchanging handshakes with the crowing baby; that was to say, the baby had grabbed one of her fingers with which she had gently touched its cheek and was doing its best to stuff it into its mouth.

'Quite right,' she said. 'Thank you.'

Rachel set a mug down on the table beside her.

'You know, I sometimes think it's so sad you and Patrick have no children of your own,' she said. 'Now that I've got Tessa I sometimes feel I'm almost perfectly happy.'

The baby was female, though to Henrietta it still remained somehow neuter.

'I believe that's the first time I've ever heard anyone say that,' she said.

'Of course, we owe it all to Patrick,' Rachel said. 'If he hadn't come along when he did, I don't suppose Simon and I would even have got married. There was Simon with his research grant at Wellford College coming to an end and no job in sight, and me having to stick at my secretary's job, or we couldn't even have afforded to go on living together. Patrick told us, I remember, that there were plenty of jobs going when he got started, but it isn't like that now. I don't know how many Simon had applied for before Patrick managed to persuade the Professor to offer him this marvellous one in his research unit. And so we could get married and have Tessa. I do think one ought to be married if one wants to have children, don't you?'

'I suppose I do,' Henrietta said. 'I've never thought much about it.'

'Haven't you missed having children yourself?' Rachel asked. 'Though perhaps that's the kind of question one shouldn't ask, I mean, if it's painful to you.'

'Perhaps it would have been once,' Henrietta said, 'but after I'd had three miscarriages I was really glad when things stopped happening.' She almost added, 'And I've got Patrick,' but she managed to stop herself in time. It would have sounded, she thought, rather too like a kind of boasting.

'I think you and Patrick would have been marvellous parents,' Rachel said. 'Did you never think of adopting?'

'Oh, we talked about it a bit, but never very seriously,' Henrietta answered. 'You and Simon are coming to our party this evening, aren't you?'

'Yes, of course.'

'You can bring Tessa in her carry-cot, and leave her in our bedroom, can't you? She'll be quite happy there.'

'I'm sure she will. But you won't mind if we're a bit late, will you? It's about the time when I feed her.'

'Come any time you like.'

'Who else is coming?'

'Most of the department, and a visiting American, and Charlie, of course.'

'Charlie . . .' Rachel said it thoughtfully, as if the name filled her with a kind of uncertainty. 'I wish I could understand him better than I do. I mean, how a man can live as he does. I feel there's something distinctly peculiar about him, and that worries me, though I know there are lots of peculiar people in universities. I wish he'd get married.'

Henrietta finished her coffee and stood up.

'I can't believe he'd make a very good husband, nice as he is in his way.'

'He isn't gay, is he?'

'I don't think he's anything, except dedicated to some obscure cardinal in the thirteenth century, who wrote some very obscure and inaccurate history—and of course to all those gadgets he loves so, his word-processors and computers and all. Well, thank you again for being so good to Patrick, and we'll see you this evening.'

Henrietta returned to the flat below, and began organizing bread and cheese and fruit for the lunch that she would have by herself, for Patrick very seldom returned home for it.

It was about four o'clock when he arrived, and set about helping Henrietta with preparations for the party. This meant moving the furniture in their sitting-room about a little, to make room for people to stand in the middle of it if that was what they wanted to do, or to sit on the various chairs that he pushed towards the walls. Then he pulled corks out of a few bottles that he had laid in so that they should be ready in case of early arrivals, and then distributed about the room the plates of canapés that Henrietta had prepared. She left him to it at that point and went to change out of the slacks and sweater that she had been wearing into a new dress that she had bought while she was in London. She was looking at herself in it in the long mirror in the bedroom, wondering if she liked it as much as she had thought she did when she bought it, when the doorbell rang.

It was much too early for a guest for the party, but it might be Rachel, coming down with some message, or perhaps Charles Hedden, or some chance visitor who would recognize the preparations for a party and would wonder why he or she had not been invited. It was not unlikely to be a nuisance, however. Henrietta waited for a little, hoping that Patrick would go to the door, but there was no sound of his doing so and the doorbell was rung again. Finishing screwing a pair of earrings to her ears, Henrietta went to answer it. She had a smile ready, assuming it would be someone she knew, but the woman who stood at the door was a stranger.

She was tall and slender, with a pale, oval face in which a pair of dark eyes burnt with a look of antagonism that was startling, in view of the fact that Henrietta had never met her before. She had wavy dark hair, cut straight above her shoulders. Her age was probably about thirty. She was wearing a dark red quilted anorak, a black skirt, and black shoes with very high heels. There was heavy make-up round her angry eyes, and thick, dark lipstick on her mouth.

'I'm Mrs Patrick Carey,' she said. 'I'm told Dr Patrick Carey lives here.'

'Oh,' Henrietta said. For the moment she could not think of anything else to say.

'Well, doesn't he?' the woman said. There was a faint Scots lilt in her voice.

'Yes, as a matter of fact, he does,' Henrietta admitted, yet she sounded doubtful about it.

'Then may I see him, please?' the woman said, but it was more like a command than a request. 'Is he in? I would be glad if I could see him without delay.'

'Yes—yes, certainly,' Henrietta said. 'Come in.'

She stood aside so that the woman could enter, then closed the door behind her.

'Patrick,' she called out, wishing that she could warn him, but not seeing how to do it. 'A visitor for you.'

He appeared at the door of the sitting-room, munching something. He had obviously been helping himself to some smoked salmon or pâté or something else that Henrietta had prepared. He smiled at the visitor.

'Yes?' he said.

'It's Dr Patrick Carey I want to see,' she said, giving Patrick a frowning look. 'He does live here, you said,' she added to Henrietta.

'This *is* Dr Patrick Carey,' she said. 'I'm awfully afraid there's been some rather terrible mistake. But come in.' She moved towards the door of the sitting-room as Patrick retreated from it. 'We must try to clear things up somehow.'

The woman advanced into the room. She stared belligerently at Patrick.

'You're not Patrick Carey,' she said. 'It's no good pretending. I know him, you know.'

'I'm afraid I am Patrick Carey,' he answered, 'and this is my wife, Henrietta. And I think you must be the woman who signs her letters E.'

'But it isn't possible,' she said, and for the first time her eyes looked puzzled and a little frightened. 'You can't be —you aren't the man I married!'

As if he were glad that that fact had been established, Patrick took her gently by the arm and led her to a chair.

'No, I'm afraid you've been the victim of a rather cruel deception,' he said, 'but I'm sure we'll be able to sort things out.'

She was still gazing at him.

'But your voice is like his, and you do look a little like him. Yes, you do. Who are you?'

'I think I'm probably the brother of the man you married,' he said. 'His real name's David.'

'And he isn't doctor anything, and he doesn't live here?'

'No.'

'But you knew all about his marrying me, didn't you, and for some rotten reason you let him use your name? What good has that done you?' The aggression was back in her voice.

'The first I knew of it, or that's to say, guessed at it, was when your first letter came, addressed to Professor Carey, at the University,' he answered. 'I had a rather awful feeling then that it might be something David had done, because I'm afraid it's the kind of person he is, but I wasn't sure of it, because the letter might not have been meant for me at all. After all, I'm not a professor. It was only when your second letter came, correctly addressed, that I began to feel certain what must have happened.'

She looked doubtful, uncertain whether to believe him.

Henrietta said, 'A thing we'd very much like to know is how you got my husband's correct address. Did someone from Knotlington get in touch with you?'

'I suppose so,' the woman answered. 'I mean, I suppose it was someone from Knotlington. I got a card yesterday, just saying, "The address you want is Dr Patrick Carey, 2 Curlingham House, Tenterfield Road, Knotlington".'

'Wasn't it signed?'

'No.'

'It was anonymous?'

'Yes.'

'What was the handwriting like?'

'It was typewritten.'

'Oh dear,' Henrietta said. 'So we're no further on with finding out who took the trouble to put you in touch with Patrick, which is rather a pity, because we think it means that someone he knows, and perhaps sees every day, believes he's a bigamist.'

'Would you tell us your name?' Patrick asked. 'I mean, apart from its being Carey.'

'It was Emma Anderson and I'm a secretary in a big shipping firm in Aberdeen. And he was ready to let me keep him once his own money ran out. He had a little when we married. But if you marry someone under a fake name, does it count?'

'I should think so, if you can prove it happened,' Patrick said, 'though I don't actually know anything about it. How long ago did this marriage take place?'

'About a month ago. And there were two witnesses, so I can prove it happened all right, if I can find him.'

'We can't help you there. We haven't the faintest idea where he is. And how long ago did he leave you?'

'About a fortnight later, saying he was only leaving for the weekend. And then he never came back.'

'But didn't you think it at all strange that a professor from a place like Knotlington should be on the loose in Aberdeen for long enough for you to get to know him well enough to marry him?'

She sighed. 'It did all happen rather in a rush. It was so—so exciting. It began just in the usual way, I mean, a pick-up in a pub, and then his moving in with me, and then me saying that this wouldn't do. I didn't really hold with it, and his saying, "Well, why don't we get married?"'

So we did, and then we went and had a grand lunch and he paid for it. And I don't know much about universities or how they manage themselves and he said he was working for a few months in Aberdeen on some sort of course, but that we'd move to Knotlington when it was over, and he's ever so educated, isn't he? And he used to go off to the University most days, though not every day, because he said it wasn't a nine to five sort of job like mine, so just what he did with himself while I was out at work I couldn't really say. But he'd usually be there when I got home in the evening, and he'd have cooked us something nice to eat. He was a fine cook. I'll say that for him.'

'So he was getting more or less free board and lodging while he was with you,' Patrick said, 'or did he buy the things for the fine meals he cooked?'

'Sometimes, but more often he got them from shops where I've got accounts. As I said, he had a little money when we married, but he said there was some trouble about getting it sent from here and so I kept him. I'm a fool, aren't I? I'm every sort of fool.'

Her face crumpled and it looked as if she was going to cry, but with an effort she controlled it, though her voice had a sob in it as she went on, 'But he's so bloody attractive. I was crazy about him. Even if he hadn't told me all those lies about himself, I'd have let him stay with me. Because they really were lies, weren't they? They really were?'

She looked from Patrick's face to Henrietta's with something in her eyes that suggested a sudden absurd hope that they would assure her that after all they had not been lies, or at least not all of them, and that she had not been quite so much of a fool after all. But at what she saw she abruptly stood up.

'Well, I'm going,' she said. 'I won't bother you any more.'

'No, don't go yet,' Patrick said. 'Stay and have a drink. We could all do with one. Whisky?'

She sank back into the chair again.

'Yes, thank you.'

He went out to the kitchen, returning after a minute or two with drinks for the three of them.

'You know, what I'm trying to think out,' he said as he gave Emma Anderson, or Carey, hers, 'is what he was getting out of being in Aberdeen. I mean, apart from enjoying your company, and getting free board and lodging.'

'Well, there was one thing he asked me to do for him when he was going away, and that was post some letters he'd written from time to time. He said they were something to do with his research.'

'And did you post them?'

'At first, but not when he didn't come back. I burnt what was left.'

'So you don't know what they were about?'

'No.'

'Perhaps he was hiding out from something, or somebody,' Henrietta suggested.

'I was wondering about that too,' Patrick said.

Emma sipped her whisky, then took a long swallow and after it gave the first hint of a smile that they had yet seen on her face.

'You're being very good to me,' she said. 'I mean, I must be quite a shock to you. D'you think I've done you any damage?'

'Damage?' Patrick said.

'Yes, for instance with that person who sent me the card with your address, who your wife says must think you've been committing bigamy. Who's your boss?'

'The head of the department I'm in is Professor Franks,' he answered. 'Professor Margaret Franks.'

'A woman.'

'Yes.'

'And did she send me that card?'

'No,' he said.

'How d'you know?'

'Because it isn't the kind of thing she'd do. If she'd written to you, she'd have signed it. She's got too much dignity
to descend to writing anonymous letters.'

'But she knows about me and that I think I'm married
to you.'

'I suppose so.'

'So I may have done you damage with her.'

'If you have, it wasn't your fault and I shouldn't dream
of blaming you.'

She nodded thoughtfully. 'The funny thing is, that's just
the kind of thing your brother would say. He's ever so
good-natured. But I really must go now.' She glanced
around the room. 'I can see you're expecting company.'
She finished her whisky and again stood up. 'Goodbye and
thanks, and I won't give you any more trouble.'

Patrick began to assure her that if there was any way in
which he and Henrietta could help her, she should let them
know, but this time she went with determination to the
door, and except that she said goodbye again to them both,
said nothing more.

When she had gone, Patrick closed the door behind her
and he and Henrietta finished their whisky and removed
their glasses to the kitchen. Returning to the sitting-room,
they both sat down, waiting in the mood of uneasy
impatience for their guests to arrive that often comes in
that lull that can occur before a party, when all preparations have been completed but no one has yet appeared.
A fear can actually make itself felt that no one is going to
appear, that there has been some hopeless mistake about
the date, even that all one's old friends have suddenly
developed an extreme hostility to one and do not mean to
appear. When the exact hour at which one has asked them
to come, in this case, six o'clock, has passed by a minute

and the doorbell has not rung, all kinds of disasters can begin to seem possible.

But at least this evening Patrick and Henrietta had something to talk about while they waited.

Henrietta began it. 'Well, what did you make of her?'

'I think David's a fool, on top of everything else,' he answered. 'At first I didn't think I was going to like her, but in the end I began to think there might be a good deal to her.'

She nodded. 'I'm beginning to feel now we oughtn't to have let her go away like that. She's family, after all. We ought to have done something more for her.'

'Don't you think we'll hear from her again?'

'I doubt it somehow. I think she's got a good deal of pride.'

'I suppose she really did marry David. The story that she did wasn't some roundabout way of getting something out of us.'

'If that's so, it was probably his idea. But I don't think so somehow. Did you notice that pretty ring she was wearing?'

'An engagement ring? No.'

'It had two opals with a small emerald between them. But she wasn't wearing it on her left hand. It was on the third finger of her right hand. But even if he hadn't given it to her and she wanted to impress us with the fact that they'd actually been married, she'd have worn it on her left hand, as if it really was an engagement ring.'

He grinned. 'That's very subtle. I'd never have thought of a thing like that.'

As he spoke the doorbell rang.

Their first guest was the American from Berkeley, Dr Heinzman. He was a very tall, very thin man of about fifty, with tight, sharp features and the kind of tan that never fades and which made the blue of his eyes look almost startlingly brilliant. He had a crop of white hair, but moved with the lounging ease of someone much younger than his years.

Accepting a glass of wine and a triangle of bread with smoked salmon on it, he remarked, 'Well, home tomorrow. And I shan't be sorry to get out of this climate of yours, though the visit has been truly rewarding. Next time, perhaps you'll be coming to us.'

'I think Robarts is the one of us you're most likely to be seeing, perhaps soon,' Patrick said. 'I'm not sure how I got the idea, but I believe he's been trying to arrange a visit to America.'

Neil Robarts and his wife were the next arrivals, and their other guests, Dr and Mrs Malcolm Mackintosh, came only a few minutes after them. But the Quinns, as Rachel had foretold, were late. Tessa, it appeared, was occupying their attention. Charles Hedden also did not appear, but no one had ever known him punctual for anything. He was as likely to come unduly early as to come late. Once, when the Careys had invited him to lunch on a Sunday to meet a visiting Italian who, apart from his scientific work, was said to have made a hobby of the study of the early Church, which they had thought would interest Charlie, he had come on the Sunday a week early. But when the party was almost complete, apart from Charlie and the Quinns, the doorbell rang again.

As they had left their front door open and most of the guests had strolled into the sitting-room as they arrived, it was faintly surprising, but Henrietta went to the door to welcome whomever it was who was too diffident to walk straight in, and there in the doorway she saw the one person who had been invited, but who she and Patrick had been sure would not come. It was Margaret Franks.

# *Three*

Margaret Franks was a tall woman, big-boned but hand-somely proportioned, with a look of strength and dominance about her that made her striking. She had strong but finely-cut features in an oval face with a pale but clear complexion that had wrinkled very little for her age and a mouth which she had touched up only with a little pale lipstick. Her eyes were grey and had a look of unusual intelligence and could express the warmest friendliness or formidable anger within moments of each other, yet could also seem to hold nothing but a chilly detachment. Her hair was light brown, curly and cut in a straight bob. As a young woman she had no doubt been beautiful, yet it was possible that she was one of those people who somehow grow into beauty as they age, for there was no question but that now at fifty she had beauty of a kind. She was dressed in a plain, well-cut grey suit that had probably cost a good deal of money, flat-heeled black shoes and she was wearing a pair of small pearl earrings which were almost certainly genuine.

Climbing the stairs just behind her was plump little Julie Bishop, her secretary, dressed in a brightly flowered blouse, a short, tight black skirt, black patterned stockings and boots with high heels. Julie had probably brought Margaret here in her car, for Margaret refused to own a car, claiming that since her home was only a few minutes' walk from the University she did not need one, and that in any case to walk instead of to drive that distance helped to keep her fit. She had very few interests outside the University, and if she should need transport to go a longer distance she had a way of discovering some friend who would drive her, as Julie had that evening, or else she would rely on a taxi, saying that this worked out far more cheaply than would the tax, the petrol, the servicing, and all that was involved in owning a car.

Yet she was by no means poor. Apart from her professor's salary, she had money that she had inherited from her father, who had been a successful surgeon in Knotlington, and she also owned the house in which she had lived with him until his death. She still lived in it, though it was unnecessarily large for a single woman with just a house-keeper to keep her company in it. But the house had belonged to her family for three or four generations. And if on the whole she spent little on herself, though she had a liking for good clothes, she was known to be generous to the odd student whom she somehow discovered to be in financial difficulties, or even to junior members of the staff of her department. When the Quinns had arrived with vir-tually no furniture of their own for the flat that they had taken, she had provided them with a table or two and a chest of drawers and some rugs from the abundance in her own large house. She had a knack of arousing strong emotions in other people, either of admiration or dislike. Patrick had begun with the one, then slid over to the other.

Henrietta did not show the surprise that she felt on seeing her, or at Margaret greeting her with a light kiss on the cheek. She then went on into the sitting-room and as Patrick came to meet her, gave him a similar greeting. He did not pretend not to be surprised at her coming. She herself never gave parties and very rarely accepted invitations to any. She would sit in the University Staff Club and drink with people in whom at the moment she was interested, usually because of their work, but it was very unusual for her to seek them out in their domestic surroundings.

'So you decided to come after all,' Patrick said. 'I didn't think it of you.'

'It isn't often that you ask me,' she said. She had a rich voice that carried remarkably, even when she was speaking quietly. 'I've let you down too often, I expect you may not believe it of me, but a roomful of people frightens me. But I particularly wanted to talk to Dr Heinzman before he left.' She turned towards the American. 'I believe you're leaving us tomorrow, Dr Heinzman.'

'That's right, Professor,' he answered. 'A few days in London, then back to California.'

'I hope you've found your visit worthwhile.'

If he had not, it had of course been largely her fault, but he was too polite to suggest that he felt this.

'Yes, indeed,' he said. 'I've had some very stimulating discussions with Patrick, and with Dr Robarts too.' Like many people, he had got quickly on to Christian name terms with Patrick, but Neil Robarts would probably still be Robarts if he knew him for ten years.

Robarts moved nearer to the group, his wife, Lydia, staying close to him. As she was taller than he was and very slim and stooped slightly, she could have a look of overhanging him. But she was a silent woman, who often seemed vaguely bewildered at what was going on around her. However, she always listened earnestly as if this might help her to understand what appeared so puzzling.

Patrick left Margaret to Dr Heinzman and the Robartses and circulated among the other guests with drinks. The Quinns had not yet appeared and Henrietta had begun to wonder if Tessa was really giving them so much trouble that perhaps they would not be able to come at all when Simon suddenly shot into the room. It was a way he had of doing almost everything, suddenly and swiftly, except when he remained oddly and stiffly motionless as if he were listening intently for something that no one but he could hear. He went into one of those nearly trance-like states as soon as he had entered the room and taken a swift look round it.

Henrietta advanced to meet him.

'It's all right, Simon,' she said. 'Rachel told me she'd be late because she'd have to deal with Tessa before she came.'

'She did, did she?' he said. 'But I thought I'd find her here. Perhaps I'd better pop upstairs and make sure things are all right. I'll be back in a minute or two.'

He turned abruptly and fled, just as Patrick was approaching him with a tray of drinks.

Though Simon was a small man and very light on his feet, they could hear him running up the stairs to the flat above. He was altogether small in his build, with a small head and a small face, a neat little nose and a narrow chin, yet he had a surprisingly wide forehead above wide-spaced blue eyes. His hair was fair and he wore it rather long, though always carefully shaped. He was dressed this evening in jeans and pullover, and with a black anorak hanging open over them. Henrietta could not remember that she had ever seen him in a suit and rather doubted if he actually possessed one.

She turned her attention to Julie Bishop, to whom Patrick had just given a glass of white wine.

'Did you drive Margaret here?' Henrietta asked. 'I hardly expected to see her.'

'That's right,' Julie said, nodding her mop of auburn curls. 'She'd never have come if I hadn't. I was just going to the car park and she was coming out of the door behind me when she said, "I suppose you're going to that party of Patrick's." And I said yes, and she said, "Christ, how I hate parties, but I suppose I'd better go. I haven't done much about that American they've been toting around. Can you take me?" So of course I said yes. And she said she didn't mean to stay long, but would I drive her home when she wanted to leave, or would I want to stay till the bitter end. So I said yes, I'd drive her home any time she wanted, and I do hope that doesn't sound rude, because you see, I thought once she got here she wouldn't want to leave any more than I would, but you know what she is. Or perhaps you don't. Sometimes I think I'm the only person in the department who really knows her.'

Henrietta thought that there was really not much truth in this, and that the two women, so totally unlike, had no understanding of one another whatever. Whether or not they liked one another was another matter. They seemed able to work together very efficiently, but it seemed impossible that two people who appeared not to share a single quality, could really know much about what went on in the other's mind.

Yet she knew that Julie was shrewder than she let herself appear and that those steely blue eyes of hers could be very penetrating. It was probable, Henrietta thought, that Julie knew far more of Margaret than Margaret did of her, though the reason for that might be that Margaret was not much interested in the woman whom she saw day after day, even though she was unlikely ever to be unkind to her. She saved her unkindness for people who in some way challenged her, such as Patrick, sometimes Neil Robarts, and sometimes even old Malcolm Mackintosh, who approached Henrietta just then, accompanied by his cheerful wife, to help themselves to things from the dish that she was carrying.

'Julie gave me some very interesting information today,' the elderly Scot told her, 'though as a matter of fact I knew it was inevitable. They're going to give Marie and me a dinner when I retire, and meanwhile they're busy collecting what they can from the rest of you in the department, and from old students and so on, to give us some smashing present. And she told us to start thinking about what we'd like, because when it comes to the point we're going to be able to choose it ourselves. And d'you know, I haven't the faintest idea about what we'd like. I feel we've already got everything we might possibly want.'

'What a splendid state of mind to be in!' Henrietta exclaimed.

'Ah, but I know what we want,' Marie Mackintosh, his wife said. 'I knew it at once when he told me what Julie

had told him, though of course I can't work out how much
of it we can buy up till I know how much money there's
actually going to be. I want a really good set of stainless
steel cutlery. I'm tired of my life of cleaning silver. And as
I realize one's income is going to go down once we're on
his pension instead of his salary, and we probably won't
be able to afford a daily woman but just someone once or
twice a week, I thought cleaning silver is one of the things
I'm going to give up. Don't you think that's sensible?'

'But our silver's beautiful,' her husband said mournfully.
'Real Georgian, some of it. It came to me from an old
grand-aunt, Hannah Clouston, whose husband made a for-
tune in shipping in Glasgow. It's really quite precious.'

'Well, we can sell it,' Marie said, 'and if the amount they
collect for us isn't enough to buy the kind of best Swedish
stainless steel I've got my eye on, we can add it to what
we've been quietly putting aside, year by year, to take us
on a trip round the world when Malcolm retires. If we
don't do it then, we'll never do it. And then we're going to
look for a cottage in the Highlands—d'you know, I've been
in Scotland only twice in my life, once to a madly dreary
scientific conference in Glasgow, and once to a wedding—'

But she was interrupted in her description of all that
they intended to do when they were able to escape from
Knotlington by the sudden appearance in the room of
Simon and Rachel Quinn, carrying Tessa in a carry-cot
between them.

Their appearance really was sudden, as Simon's so often
were, though perhaps this time it seemed to be so only
because of the howl that Tessa gave on finding herself in a
roomful of strangers whose appearance seemed not to please
her. There was a general movement in the room towards
her, to murmur admiration, to win a smile from her.

Margaret Franks was the one person who showed no sign
of being aware that something so special as a baby had
been brought into the room, but went on holding Dr

Heinzman firmly in conversation, though he had lifted a hand to click his fingers at Tessa and did not look as if he were listening very attentively to Margaret. Henrietta could not help wondering if she was being so voluble out of a desire to make up for her far from kind treatment of him earlier in his visit, or if she was imposing herself on him with a kind of malicious dominance, making him feel her presence whether he wanted to or not.

'Where shall we put her, Henrietta?' Rachel asked.

'Come along, I'll show you,' Henrietta answered, and led the way to the bedroom. There was a second bedroom in the flat, that contained a spare bed, but also a table strewn with books and papers that belonged to Patrick. An occasional visitor slept there, but mostly it was used by him as what, for reasons best known to himself, he refused to call a study.

'Will she be all right in here?' Henrietta asked.

'Yes, fine,' Simon answered. 'Perhaps if you'd draw the curtains . . .'

Henrietta went to the window to draw them, but as she reached up she suddenly paused.

'Oh, look,' she said. 'That looks like a fire, doesn't it?'

They joined her, looking out into the darkness of the wintry evening.

At some distance away, in the direction of the centre of the town, there was a red glow in the sky, quite unlike the general pale illumination that came from the long avenues of street lamps.

'It does, doesn't it?' Rachel said. 'And it can't be far from the University.'

'Perhaps one of our noble buildings has gone up in flames,' Simon suggested, but there was an unusual shrillness in his voice, as if the thought excited him. 'Anyway, it's something quite big.'

'Well, we don't have to do anything about it.' Henrietta

jerked the curtains together. 'Tessa's really going to be quite happy here, is she?'

'I'll stay with her for a little,' Simon said, 'just till she goes to sleep.'

'I'll bring you a drink, then,' Henrietta said, and returned with Rachel to the sitting-room.

When she returned to the bedroom with the drink for Simon she found him still at the window, peering out between the curtains, which he had pulled a little apart, but hearing her come in he let them fall and thanked her for the drink.

'Anyway, it can't be the department,' he said. 'It's too near. It might be the Engineering building or even the Library.'

'Oh, I don't think so,' Henrietta said. 'It's too near even for them.' She looked down at the baby. 'She's asleep now, isn't she?'

'Yes, but I'll stay with her a little longer,' Simon said. She left him, feeling fairly sure that once she was gone he would turn back to the window to gaze at the red glow in the darkness as if it was a show of fireworks.

However, he came into the sitting-room after only a few minutes and helped himself hungrily to a taramasalata dip, as if it were a long time since he had last eaten. But Simon generally looked like that when food was put before him. He always ate with a greedy sort of speed, which had made Henrietta wonder, when she had first observed it, just how he had been brought up. She still knew very little about this, except that he had been the only son of not very successful theatrical parents, who had generally left him in the care of his mother's father when they were touring, an old man to whom he appeared to have been devoted, though Simon had had to take as much care of him as he ever had of Simon. His parents now were somewhere in Australia, and his grandfather was dead. Simon's protective love of his child, Henrietta was inclined to believe, came at least partly

from a determination that her childhood should be as different as possible from his own.

The evening went on pleasantly in a quiet way with Dr
Heinzman the first to leave, after thanking Margaret Franks
with restrained dignity for the great pleasure he had experi-
enced during his visit to Knotlington and the profitable
contacts that he had made there. Then, in the small hall
of the flat, he had thanked Patrick and Henrietta with more
sincerity for their hospitality, and turned to the door, with
Patrick preparing to see him down the stairs. But the door
was as far as they got, for as they reached it pounding
footsteps could be heard on the stairs below them, and
Charlie Hedden came panting up to them. He was the one
person whom they had expected that evening who had not
appeared. He was a tall, gaunt man with a long, fleshy
nose, a cleft chin and thick grey hair.

'Is she here—Professor Franks?' he gasped. 'They've
been hunting for her everywhere, and then suddenly I
thought she might be here.' But without waiting for an
answer, he thrust his way into the sitting-room. He strode
across it to where Margaret stood, talking now to Neil
Robarts and his wife. 'Professor, your house in on fire!' he
cried. 'They're all there, firemen, police, and an ambulance,
but there's nothing they can do. It's practically burnt to
the ground.'

With a look of horror on her face, Margaret exclaimed, 'An
ambulance! You don't mean Mrs Digby was in the house!'

Mrs Digby was the housekeeper who had worked for
Margaret's father for twenty years before his death, and
had stayed on after it to look after Margaret.

'I don't know!' Charles Hedden answered. 'I don't know
if anyone was in it. The ambulance may have been just in
case of some emergency. As a matter of fact, I'm not sure
it was an ambulance. I didn't stay to stare at things when
I saw whose house it was, I went looking for you. I thought

you might be in your department, and when I found you weren't, I looked in the Staff Club, and then the Library. Then I suddenly thought of this party the Careys were giving and that you might possibly be here.'

'She can't have been in the house,' Margaret said, her deep voice pitched higher than normal. 'She always spends Saturday evenings with her sister and they go to the cinema together.'

If it was true that her house was burnt to the ground, as Charles Hedden had said, that in itself seemed for the moment to be of almost no consequence to Margaret.

'Will someone drive me down there?' she asked the room at large.

Julie Bishop was beginning to say that of course she would, when Patrick said, 'I'll take you down.'

He took Margaret by the arm and hurried her towards the door. There was a general movement towards it and a bustling of people trying to pass one another down the stairs. Only Rachel Quinn did not make for them, but went swiftly into the bedroom, coming out after a moment with Tessa in her arms and hurrying up the stairs instead of down them.

Henrietta stood in the middle of the deserted room, wondering what she ought to do. Patrick and Margaret were too far in advance of all the other people for her to be able to join them. But as she hesitated there, Simon came up to her and said, 'Come along, we'd better go too. The Professor's going to need help when the shock of it really hits her.'

'That fire we saw from the window . . .' Henrietta said, but she let herself be guided out of the room, grabbing a coat from a peg in the hall as they passed and struggling into it. 'Of course, we ought to have thought it was just about where Margaret's house is, but I never thought . . . I never dreamt . . .'

THY BROTHER DEATH 57

'Nor did I,' Simon said. 'The houses of the people one knows don't get burnt to the ground.'

'But whatever can have started it?'

Simon's car, an old and shabby Citroën that he had managed to buy very cheaply, was in the garage attached to the house, and by the time they had reached it and driven out to the street the other cars that had been left parked in the street were already gone.

Starting off after them with Henrietta in the seat beside him, Simon said, 'A gas explosion, an electrical fault, arson.'

'Arson! You mean it could have been started deliberately!'

'That happens, doesn't it? Not that it's likely, but kids can do stupid things that get out of hand. What's meant to be just a bit of vandalism that's one hell of a joke and nothing more, turns into a major disaster.'

'At least losing her home won't be such a very major disaster for Margaret,' Henrietta said. 'That's something to be thankful for.'

He gave her a quick sidelong glance. 'What do you mean?'

'Just that it's been a sort of white elephant to her ever since her father died. And I don't think she'd be much inclined to love a mere house, even if she'd lived in it all her life. But perhaps I'm wrong.'

'No, I think you're probably right. Anyway, let's hope its insured.'

Simon turned into the main road at the bottom of Tenterfield Road and sped on in the direction of the red glow that they could see plainly in the sky.

A strange, thick darkness hung above it, seeming to be far darker than the mere darkness of the evening, and which could only be the smoke above the burning building. It was on the main road and had been cordoned off by the police, who were diverting traffic down a side-street near it. Simon

found that he was unable to approach close to the fire, but
he was able to park in a small side-street just before they
reached it and he and Henrietta got out of the car and
walked towards the blaze.

The house was one of the problems of which everyone in
Margaret Franks's department had heard. They knew that
she had made a few attempts to sell it, but that they had
been unsuccessful. One of the difficulties about it was that
it was a listed building. That it had been declared one was
something that had been achieved by her father and of
which he was exceedingly proud. It had been built about
the middle of the nineteenth-century, and was a specimen
of the fashion for the neo-Gothic that had possessed people
at that time. It was only of moderate size, yet it had a
turret or two, an entrance under a pointed Gothic archway,
battlements and small, secret-looking windows through
which it was possible to imagine that a visitor might be
greeted by a well-aimed arrow.

However, it was not built of stone, but of the dull red
brick that never weathers and that had been much in use
at the time of its construction. For most of the twentieth
century it had been regarded as an unfortunate monstrosity,
but disciples of Sir John Betjeman had rescued it from
ignominy and for some years it had been among the buildings in the town considered to be of too much historic and
aesthetic value to be allowed to suffer any restoration,
except what was absolutely necessary for its preservation.
Margaret Franks, unable to sell it, because for one thing
its size was awkward, not large enough to be turned into
offices or something institutional, yet of an inconvenient
size to be lived in by anyone who could not afford a staff
of servants, would have liked to have had it pulled down
and something small and comfortable built in its place. But
she had not been able to do this because of that irritating
business of its being a listed building. Its only advantage
for her was that it was close to the University.

Inside, it was atrociously inconvenient. It had no central heating, its one bathroom was a surprisingly large room through which bitter draughts somehow found their way at all times of the year and in which a very large bath with a mahogany surround stood in the middle. The kitchen was dank and cheerless with a coke stove for heating the hot water, the only concession to modernity being a gas cooking stove, though the old black kitchen range still occupied most of one wall. Of course, the fact that all these things had not been rectified was undoubtedly Margaret's own fault. She could easily have afforded to make the place tolerably comfortable. But she had always held that to spend money on it would be a sheer waste, since sooner or later she would be sure to leave it. The site, so near the centre of the town, would be exceedingly valuable, if only the wretched building could be got out of the way, or if only some madman would arrive in Knotlington and fall in love with it.

As Henrietta and Simon walked together towards the fire, which they could smell now, the acrid tang of burning filling the evening air, Henrietta said, 'You know, one could almost suppose it was a friend of Margaret's who set the place on fire. Once she's got used to the thought of it, she'll probably be immensely thankful it's gone.'

'Always supposing Mrs Digby wasn't in it,' Simon said.

They were walking fast, and they could now feel some heat being wafted towards them. The stench of the burning was growing stronger.

'Don't!' Henrietta said. 'That isn't possible.'

He did not answer.

After a moment she said excitedly, 'It isn't possible, is it? Didn't Margaret say Mrs Digby always goes to the cinema with her sister on a Saturday evening? It isn't possible, Simon.'

'Who knows?' he said. 'People sometimes change their habits. Perhaps the old woman set the place on fire herself by doing something stupid with the electricity. And Charlie said there was an ambulance there.'

This time it was Henrietta who did not answer. It was in silence that they reached the point at which a policeman stopped them and told them that they had better not try to go any further.

From where they stood they could see the burning building, a skeleton of itself standing gauntly among flames. Flames came licking out of the narrow windows and rose above the battlements. When Charlie Hedden had said that the house had been burnt to the ground he had not described accurately what had happened. The roof appeared to have crashed in and the door naturally to have disappeared, but the red brick was most of it still standing stoutly, sprayed by the hoses of the firemen who had to keep at some distance from it because of the intense heat. In the light from the flames, and in their helmets and uniforms, they looked curiously small and dark and not quite human. Several fire-engines were drawn up near the house. An ambulance too stood at a little distance from it. Besides people who had gathered outside the roped-off area to share in the excitement, there were police spread out along the edges of it. Standing within it, side by side and gazing silently at the scene of destruction were Margaret Franks and Patrick.

As Henrietta watched she saw Margaret suddenly turn away from Patrick and thrust her way through the crowd towards a telephone-box across the street from the house. People stood aside so that she could pass, looking at her with an almost superstitious air of curiosity, as if she herself had some kind of responsibility for having brought the blaze into being. Patrick, who had seen Henrietta and Simon, came towards them.

'What's she doing?' Henrietta asked as he joined them. 'Who's she phoning?'

'Mrs Digby's sister,' Patrick answered. 'She wants to make sure that Mrs Digby's with her.'

'Haven't the firemen told her yet if there's anyone in the house?' Simon said.

'They haven't been able to get inside it yet,' Patrick replied. 'They've tried, but the heat's driven them off. I imagine that actually Mrs Digby is sitting safely in some cinema somewhere, never dreaming that all she's ever possessed has gone up in flames.'

'Aren't they going to be able to save anything?' Henrietta asked.

'Not much, anyway. I've been talking to a police inspector, or someone who seems to be in charge. And the few witnesses they've got, so he said, agree that the place seemed just to burst into flames all of a sudden.'

'As if a bomb had gone off?' It seemed to Henrietta as Simon spoke that there was a kind of eagerness in his voice and his face had the pallor of excitement.

'A gas explosion, I should think,' Patrick said.

'I suppose they haven't any theory about that yet,' Henrietta said. 'I wonder how long it'll take them to get it under control—' She broke off as she saw Margaret emerge from the telephone-box. 'Look, I think she's had good news, she doesn't look too upset.'

'Thank God for that,' Simon said. 'And if it's all right with you, I'll go home now. I ought to let Rachel know what's been happening.' He turned to Henrietta. 'They'll bring you home, won't they, or d'you want to come back with me now?'

'We'll bring her home,' Patrick said. 'Well, Margaret, what's the situation?'

'It's all right,' Margaret said in a surprisingly calm voice as Simon left them. 'She's with her sister, having tea. They were going to a cinema, but of course they called that off when I told her what had happened. She's very upset at hearing that probably all her clothes and everything have gone, but she's going to spend the night at her sister's and we'll meet in the morning.'

'What are you doing yourself tonight?' Patrick asked.

'I think you'd better come home with us,' Henrietta said. 'Will you do that? Our spare room's not very grand but the bed's comfortable, so I've been told, and we can get it ready for you in a few minutes.'

'That's very good of you,' Margaret said. 'Yes, I'll be very grateful if I can do that.'

'And I think we might as well go now,' Patrick said. 'We can't do any good here.'

'Only we'd better tell the police where to find me, hadn't we?' Margaret said. 'That man we talked to before . . .' She pointed. 'There he is.'

Patrick set off towards the tall figure standing talking to a fireman beside one of the fire-engines.

Coming back after he had spoken to the two men for a moment, he said, 'They think they'll be able to get inside the house fairly soon. I've told them where they can find you and given them our telephone number. Come along.'

The three of them set off towards where Patrick had left his car.

As she dropped into the seat beside Patrick and Henrietta climbed into the back seat, Margaret seemed suddenly to lose her self-control. She bent forward, taking her head in her hands and beginning to shake all over. An odd little sound came from between her lips, not quite a moan or a sob, but very near to it. Neither Patrick nor Henrietta spoke. After a minute or two Margaret drew her breath in and let it out again in a deep sigh and settled back in her seat, the trembling gradually ceasing. She was trying hard to acquire that self-control that she had momentarily lost. All the same, when they reached Curlingham House and got out of the car, she took hold of Patrick by the arm and let him lead her up the stairs to the Careys' flat.

It was littered with the remains of the party. Empty

glasses stood about and plates on which remains of half-eaten biscuits and sandwiches had been left. Henrietta automatically began to clean up the mess, but Patrick said, 'Don't bother about that. A drink first for all of us, I think.'

The gas fire was still alight and Margaret dropped into a chair beside it. She leant back and let out another gasping sigh. Patrick poured out whisky for the three of them and although the way that her nerves had taken Henrietta was to make her itch to tidy the room, she accepted her glass and sat down in a low chair facing Margaret.

She gulped some whisky, then, her voice unusually hoarse, remarked, 'You're being very good to me.'

She sounded as if this surprised her. Her eyes, dwelling on Patrick as he also found a chair for himself, had a look in them which Henrietta from time to time had seen before and which she always found disturbing and rather sad. In some way it seemed to convey a feeling in Margaret that only she herself and he were in the room and that Henrietta simply was not there.

'I haven't even begun to take in what it's going to mean to me,' Margaret went on. 'I'll have to begin by buying some clothes, but tomorrow's Sunday, so I shan't be able to do much till the day after.'

'Don't try thinking about that sort of thing yet,' Patrick said. 'We can manage for you somehow.'

'I can lend you a nightdress,' Henrietta said, 'though it'll be a bit short for you. And Patrick's pyjamas will be a bit long.'

'That's all right, I've slept naked before,' Margaret said, 'and I don't want to be a lot of trouble to you.'

'You must stay as long as you want to,' Patrick said.

'Oh, I won't want to impose on you,' she answered, and then, half under her breath went on, ' "Ladybird, ladybird, fly away home. Your house is on fire, all your children are gone . . ." D'you know, it's only just occurred to me, but my children *are* gone, nearly the whole lot. Oh God, what a horrible thought!'

'Your *children?*' Patrick said, puzzled. 'Oh, I see what you mean—your notes, your papers.'

'Yes, they're my children, the only ones I'll ever have.'

'Did you really have a lot of them in the house?' he said. 'Weren't they mostly in the department?'

'No, unfortunately. I used to take them home in the evenings and work on them there. Work! My God, how I always worked! There were six or seven years' work in that house. I suppose I can reproduce most of it, but it'll take me an age. That book I was going to write, that I'd even got a contract for. Did you know I'd actually signed a contract for the thing, and even got taken out to lunch by a publisher on the strength of it? No more lunches now, I'm afraid. No book. Not one. What a disaster!' She began to laugh. She might have meant to sound as if she were actually cheered by the thought that the book that she had planned need after all never be written, but there was hysteria in the tone of it.

Henrietta found that she could not stay still any longer, and began to tidy the room. Then she made up the bed for Margaret, then she made some sandwiches and coffee and put them on a tray to take into the sitting-room for their supper. While she was doing it Patrick and Margaret talked quietly, first about the notes that had been destroyed, then about other aspects of their work and about affairs in the department. No one who had heard them could have dreamt that there had ever been any hostility in their relationship. Henrietta took a good deal of pride in Patrick's sensitivity and kindness. She came and went about the flat as unobtrusively as she could, leaving him to cope with the wounds of the woman for whom at times he expressed the bitterest enmity.

It was about ten o'clock when the sandwiches had been eaten, the coffee drunk and Margaret was talking of going to bed, then saying that it was perhaps too soon, because she knew that she would not be able to sleep at all, and then almost immediately saying that she was so tired that if they did not mind she would go to her room at once, when the doorbell rang.

Patrick went to answer it, returning to the sitting-room with two men whom he introduced as Detective-Inspector Brightmore and Detective-Sergeant Dance. Henrietta recognized the Inspector as the tall man to whom Patrick had spoken before he and Henrietta and Margaret had left the scene of the fire. He looked about forty and had a hard-looking body with wide shoulders and unusually long arms. His face had the kind of thinness that made it seem haggard, with small, deep-set dark eyes. The Sergeant, though not so tall, looked far the more powerful and was perhaps ten years the younger.

Both men were in raincoats and there was something about their bearing that made Henrietta feel that had she met them in the street, far removed from any kind of crisis, she would immediately have recognized them as police.

Margaret had come to her feet as they entered the room.

'Is it out? she demanded.

'The fire? Oh, I'm afraid not, Professor,' the Detective-Inspector said. 'That's something that may not happen till the morning. But we're getting it under control. The firemen have managed to get inside and we've come here to tell you two things that I think you'll find disturbing. We wouldn't have troubled you tonight if it hadn't been that we've some very urgent questions to ask about them. To begin with, we're almost certain that the cause of the fire was arson.'

Her face went curiously blank, as if the word had no meaning for her.

'Arson,' he repeated. 'We think it was started deliberately.'

'You don't mean it,' she said. 'Who'd do such a thing?'

'Perhaps you'll be able to tell us something that may help to answer that question,' he said. 'But there's been petrol liberally spilled about the house. Of course, it's mostly been burnt up already, but there are traces of it here and there in places where the fire hadn't yet got a hold.'

'You said there were two things you wanted to tell Professor Franks,' Patrick said. 'What's the other thing?'

The two detectives exchanged a look which suggested that neither of them was anxious to reply, but the Inspector went on.

'In the room which I believe must have been your lounge,' he said, 'on the ground floor, though it's now pretty completely gutted, there's the body of a woman. It's so badly burnt that I can't give you much description of her, but we think she was a young woman, fairly tall and fairly slim. Did you know that there was anyone in your house?'

Margaret's face had gone a sickly white. For a moment Henrietta thought that she might faint. But she managed to stay erect and stiff.

'No, there was no one there at all,' she said. 'Mrs Digby was with her sister.'

'Isn't the Mrs Digby whom you told us about an elderly woman?' the Inspector asked.

'Yes, yes, of course. But you say there's a woman there in the house—dead—burnt alive? It isn't possible!'

'I'm sorry to have to tell you something so distressing,' he said, 'but I'm afraid it's true. But have you no idea who she might be?'

'None—none at all! Whoever she was, she shouldn't have been there. She'd no right to be there. Are you going to be able to identify her?'

'We've only one thing to go on at present,' he replied. 'This. It wasn't damaged by the fire.'

He held out a hand. In the palm of it there was a gold ring. It was set with two opals with a small emerald between them.

# Four

Henrietta looked at Patrick. He was looking at her with his eyebrows raised questioningly. She remembered then that he had not noticed the ring on the hand of the woman who had visited them that afternoon.

'Was it on her hand?' she asked.

'On the dead woman's?' Inspector Brightmore said. 'Yes.'

'Well, I think we've seen it. That is, I've seen it, I'm not sure that my husband did. We had a visitor in the afternoon, a woman who said she was from Aberdeen—'

'Aberdeen?' Margaret Franks interrupted sharply.

It reminded Henrietta that Margaret, like most of the other people in the Department of Biochemistry, had seen the letter addressed to a nonexistent Professor Carey, which most of them apparently had thought was probably meant for Patrick.

'So she said,' Henrietta went on, but paused looking helplessly at Patrick, not knowing how much he wanted to tell the police about their visit.

He took up the story. 'Yes, we'd never met her before, but she introduced herself as my sister-in-law. I've a brother, David, who married her about a month ago. He hadn't told us anything about it, but there's nothing odd in that. We hear very little of him. At the moment we don't even know where he is. But she had our address and came to see us, and we've got her home address. She said she was a secretary, working for a shipping company, and her name had been Emma Anderson.'

'You've her address?' the Inspector said.

'Yes. If you'll excuse me for a moment . . .' Patrick made for the door.

Henrietta knew that he had the second letter from the woman from Aberdeen in the wallet in his pocket, but she realized that he did not intend to show it to the police. Leaving the room, he returned after a minute or two with his address book in his hand, in which he must hastily have written down the address that was at the head of the letter.

'Here it is,' he said. 'I made a note of it. 12 Birdway Gardens, Aberdeen. But apart from that ring, have you no evidence of who this dead woman was?'

'Not so far,' the Inspector answered.

'The ring may not be unique. She may not have been my sister-in-law at all.'

'That's always possible. But the design's unusual.' The Inspector had handed Patrick's address book to Sergeant Dance, who was making a note of the Aberdeen address. 'And her husband—your brother—you say you don't know where he is at the moment?'

'I'm afraid not.'

'But his usual address is Aberdeen, is it?'

'I'm not even sure of that. The woman who came to see us didn't stay for long and didn't tell us much about herself or my brother.'

'Did she tell you what she was doing in Knotlington?'

'No, except that she'd wanted to meet us. My brother's pretty much of an eccentric, Inspector. I dare say she just wanted to see what sort of relations he had.'

For the present, Henrietta realized, Patrick was doing his best to protect David and not to state that it looked as if he had simply deserted his wife and that she had been trying to trace him.

In a voice that was very unsteady, she asked, 'Was she actually burnt to death?'

'We think it was probably the smoke that killed her,' Brightmore answered. 'But the flames had got to her before we found her and destroyed most of her clothing and her hair. She'd apparently broken a window, trying to get out, but was overcome before she could manage it.'

'But what was she doing in my house at all?' Margaret demanded. She demanded it loudly, as if she felt that her presence was being ignored and that it was time that someone paid attention to her. 'Did you send her there, Patrick?'

'Of course not,' he said.

'Well, what was she doing there?'

'I haven't the least idea.'

'Inspector, I've a suggestion to make,' she said. 'It's that I should ring up my housekeeper, Mrs Digby, who's spending the night at her sister's and ask her if she let this woman into my house. I can't imagine why she should have done so, but if she didn't, I don't know how a complete stranger got in.'

'She's a complete stranger to you, is she, Professor?'

'I'd never even heard of her until Dr Carey spoke of her a few minutes ago.'

'Very well then, if you'd do as you suggest, it might be helpful.'

The telephone was in the hall. Patrick led Margaret to it, then, returning to the sitting-room, closed the door on her.

'She said nothing to us about going to see Professor Franks,' he said. 'I'm sorry we can tell you so little about her.'

'But she did ask you who your boss was,' Henrietta said, 'and you told her the head of your department was Professor Franks. We don't know what was in her mind when she asked that, and why was she trying to get out of the room by the window instead of by the door? Was it already on fire? Didn't she have any warning?'

Margaret came back into the room and stood still just inside the door.

'Mrs Digby let her in,' she said. She had an angry look on her face, as if she had just been quarrelling with her absent housekeeper. Crossing the room, she dropped into the chair where she had been sitting earlier. 'She said the woman came about five o'clock and wanted to see me. Mrs Digby said I wasn't in, so the woman asked when she expected me. Mrs Digby said I'd probably be home by six o'clock, and like a fool Mrs Digby let her in and when it was time for her to catch the bus to go to her sister's, she told the woman that she'd got to go and would leave her, but that I was sure to be in soon. That may not be as odd as it sounds. People do drop in to see me from time to time whom she doesn't know and she knows I don't mind it if she leaves them in the living-room. But of course they're people whom I do know, not complete strangers. However, the woman's respectability seems to have reassured her, particularly as she mentioned having been given my address by Dr Carey.'

'But didn't Mrs Digby know you'd be coming to our party at six o'clock?' Henrietta asked.

'I may not have mentioned it to her,' Margaret said, 'or if I did, she may not have thought I'd really come. I don't often go to parties.'

'So this Mrs David Carey was there alone in the house when the fire started,' Brightmore said.

'And you still haven't answered my wife's question,' Patrick said. 'The living-room's on the ground floor, isn't it? Why didn't she dash out by the door as soon as she smelled fire, instead of breaking a window?'

Sergeant Dance cleared his throat, as if he were about to speak, but a glance from the Inspector silenced him.

'I was coming to that,' the Inspector said. 'By the time we were able to get in, the door of that room was burnt to ashes, but the lock was lying there among them. Being metal, it hadn't suffered much. And it was locked. Locked apparently on the outside of the door. The key was still in the lock. Do you understand that, Professor? The woman seems to have been locked into the room, and breaking a window was her only way of getting out of it. But as I said, the smoke overcame her before she managed it. Would your Mrs Digby have locked her in when she had to leave her to go and catch her bus and you hadn't returned? Would that have been a normal precaution for her to take, leaving someone there who was a stranger to her?'

Margaret did not answer for a moment, but her face became a chalky white. For the first time since she had heard of the fire, it stiffened with a look of deep horror.

'Do you realize what you're saying, Inspector?' she said in a quiet but hoarse voice.

'I'm just asking a question,' he said.

'Would Mrs Digby . . . ? No, of course she wouldn't. But why don't you ask her yourself?

'I was coming to that. I'd be grateful for her sister's address. We'll go out and see her presently. However, you're sure she wouldn't have left the visitor locked into your living-room?'

'Certainly she wouldn't.'

'Yet somebody turned the key.'

She pressed a hand against her forehead, then drew it slowly down over her face, as if to obliterate any expression that might have remained on it.

'Yes,' she said quietly, 'if you say so. You're quite sure of it, are you?'

'At the moment I feel inclined to say yes, but it's possible, when the fire's out and we can examine the results of it more thoroughly, we'll find we've made some mistake.'

'But you believe that whoever lit the fire not only committed arson, but murder too.'

He did not answer, except to give a slight nod of his head, then he went on, 'We think the fire was started in several places in the house at more or less the same time, and that whoever did it got away from the house by the door from the basement into the yard, and the lane at the back of the house. There's no sign that the bolt there had

been pushed to, and the key hadn't been turned in the lock.
Whether or not he got in that way we don't know. The
front door's burnt, but the lock on it is only a Yale and
would have sprung open naturally when the door collapsed.
But I'd be interested to know, Professor, whether anyone
besides yourself and Mrs Digby ever had a key to that door.
It won't tell us much, I'm afraid, but all the same I'd be
interested to know.'

'Not that I know of,' she said. 'I never gave my key to
anyone that I can remember. And you'd better ask Mrs
Digby herself whether or not she ever did.'

'Was there no spare key anywhere? You didn't, for
instance, leave your key with a neighbour in case you happened to lock yourself out one day? A lot of people do that.'

She gave a slow shake of her head. 'I'm not on those
sort of terms with my neighbours. On one side they're
Buddhists, and they spend a lot of time chanting at a
window facing my house and it really drives me mad when
I'm trying to work. I've protested, but it hasn't done any
good. And on the other side there's a furniture restorers',
which is shut morning and evening. So it wouldn't be much
use leaving a key with them. But isn't it fairly easy to force
a spring lock? One reads about its being done with a strip
of plastic. Couldn't whoever got into the house have done
it that way?'

'It's possible. But that brings us to another question. I
realize, of course, what an intense shock you've suffered
this evening, and that you may not be able yet to think
very clearly about it, but can you tell us of anyone who
could conceivably have wanted to burn your house to the
ground? Forget about the poor woman who died in the fire
for the moment. She might have been just a hazard he
hadn't expected to encounter when he started the blaze.
He may have known you were coming to a party here and
that Mrs Digby would be out, and therefore may have
assumed that the house would be empty. Then perhaps,

when she smelled smoke, the strange woman did come out
of the room and came face to face with him as he went
through the house, spilling his petrol, and so could have
identified him if he'd let her get away. He might then have
pushed her back into the room she'd come out of and turned
the key on her. But can you think of anyone, have you any
suspicion, can you help us at all with any suggestion, of
who might have done such a thing to you as burn your
house?'

She stared at him hard but sightlessly, then gave a violent
shudder.

'No!' she said. 'No! There are plenty of people who have
it in for me. I know that. I've never gone out of my way
to propitiate people. I've made enemies. There are plenty of
enemies in the university world. Patrick Carey there almost
hates me. We were friends once, but he can't endure the
fact that I've got a certain amount of power over him. He
can't endure that from anyone. Are the police like that too?
People are bound to hate you if you've got power. Oh yes,
Dr Carey hates me. And there are others . . . But to burn
my house down—no, that isn't the sort of thing they'd do.'

Patrick spoke gently. 'I didn't burn your house down,
Margaret. And I'm not a murderer. And I've an alibi, if
you've any doubts about me. Henrietta and I were here
together all the afternoon.'

'I don't believe the alibis that husbands and wives give
each other are taken very seriously, are they, Inspector?'
Henrietta said. 'But this time it happens to be true.'

'And in any case you're thinking that I burnt the house
down myself, to get the insurance money,' Margaret said.
'I've an alibi too. I spent the whole day in the Department
of Biochemistry, from about nine in the morning until about
six o'clock in the evening, and you'll find plenty of people
who'll confirm that. It's true I had lunch in the Staff Club,
but you'll find people who were there who'll confirm that
too. And then Miss Julie Bishop drove me here.'

'Of course your house is insured?' the Inspector said.
'Certainly.'

'But to return to the matter of Mrs Emma Carey, if that's
who the dead woman was,' he said, and looked at Patrick,
'there's a question to be asked. Was she killed, as I suggested just now, because if she'd escaped she could have
identified the arsonist, or was the house set on fire to conceal
the manner of her death? Now, we won't keep you any
longer. I think we'll go on to see Mrs Digby. We may call
in again on you tomorrow with more questions and perhaps
more information, but I think we've done all we can for
the present. Thank you for your help. Good night.'

The Sergeant also muttered good night and after Margaret had given them the address of Mrs Digby's sister, the
two men left the flat.

Patrick followed them to the front door and closed it after
them as they left. When he returned to the room Margaret
was leaning back in her chair with her eyes closed. But
there was no sign of relaxation about her. The furrows on
her forehead suggested that she had closed her eyes only
to be able to think more intently of something than would
be possible if she had to take notice of her surroundings.

Suddenly her eyes opened. 'You know a lot more than
you told that policeman, don't you, Patrick?' she said. 'That
brother of yours, why have you never told me anything
about him before?'

'I'm sure I have,' he said. 'I may not have said much
about him. There was no reason why I should. But I'm
sure you knew I had a brother.'

'You may have mentioned him,' she said. 'I can't swear
that you haven't. But you've never said much about him.
Why is that?'

'As I said, there was no reason why I should,' he
answered.

'And no reason why you should say so little about him

to those men, when his wife's just been burnt to death in my house? What's that going to mean to him?'

'I wish I knew.'

'Do you really not know where he is?'

He looked at Henrietta. 'Shall we tell her the whole story?'

'So there is a story?' Margaret said.

'Part of one,' he answered. 'We can't actually tell you the whole of it, because we don't know it ourselves, but you were right that we kept a bit back from those detectives, which may have been a mistake. I expect we'll have to tell them the rest of it sooner or later, unless we hear from my brother. This is all going to get into the newspapers, isn't it, and that may flush him out from wherever he is. What d'you think, Henrietta? Shall I go on?'

'I think that might be best,' she replied. 'It's all bound to come out sometime.'

He walked away towards the window, and held a curtain a little aside, gazing out into the darkness. If he could see any of the remains of the blaze he did not speak of it, but let the curtain fall again and stayed with his back to the window.

'D'you remember a letter that came a few days ago for someone called Professor Carey?' he asked.

'Yes,' Margaret said.

'And I said it had nothing to do with me. I wasn't a professor, and what happened to it then I don't know, but I believe it went the round of the department. Perhaps you saw it yourself.'

'Yes,' she said again.

'Well, what did you make of it?'

'Nothing much. I couldn't make any special sense of it.'

'It didn't make you think I'd committed bigamy and was keeping a second wife in Aberdeen?'

'I'm not a complete idiot. No.'

'Are you sure?'

'Don't be an utter fool, Patrick. Of course I never thought anything of the kind.'

'Well, someone, probably in the department, did think that that was the explanation of the letter, or at least that it might be, and took the matter seriously enough to think it worth sending an anonymous letter to Aberdeen, giving the woman who signed herself E. my correct title and address. I knew that because I received a letter from her here yesterday morning, which came to this flat. And it appeared that she believed she was married to me and that I ought to be sending her money. Henrietta and I didn't know what to do about it, but we assumed that my brother had been up to something, and to explain why we thought that, I'd better tell you a little about him.'

He sat down on the sofa where Henrietta had also sat, and put an arm round her shoulders. She was feeling almost intolerably tired and was glad to lean against him, but she could feel that it was he who was holding on to her for support.

'It isn't a pleasant kind of thing to have to say about one's brother,' he went on. 'And I've never entirely managed to overcome a kind of affection for him. But he's a pathological liar for one thing, and we think possibly a crook. Not that we actually know much about how he's really kept himself, but we've assumed it hasn't been honestly. He stayed in Kenya with my father until his death, then got through all that my father had left him in a very short time, then came to England and got what he could out of me before I caught on to the kind of person he'd turned into. We hadn't seen anything of each other since we were quite young, you see. But he'd tell us he'd some sort of job and give us an address, but if we wrote to the address he'd always have moved on, and if we tried to trace him through the job, it'd turn out they'd never heard of him. So when it began to look as if someone had married a woman called E. in my name, it seemed fairly reasonable to assume that it was David who'd done it.'

'And she came here to see you today, did she?' Margaret asked.

He nodded. 'She came here, demanding to see Dr Patrick Carey, but when I appeared she stated that I certainly wasn't the man she'd married. She didn't stay long, and she didn't tell us what she intended to do next, though we told her to keep in touch with us if there was any way we could help her. There's no doubt at all it was David whom she'd married only a few weeks ago. What he was doing in Aberdeen we don't know. He seems to have had a little money when he arrived there, but to have been quite happy to live on her when the money ran out. He told her he was doing some course at the University there and she believed him. Then he left for what he said was a weekend, but he never went back, so today, after she'd had this anonymous letter from someone here, she came looking for him.'

'And for some reason, when she failed to find him here, she came straight to see me,' Margaret said. 'What do you make of that?'

'I haven't any idea why she did it,' Patrick answered.

'She didn't say why she was going to?'

'No. She didn't even say anything about it.'

She stretched her arms out and gave a great yawn, then stood up.

'Well, thank you for the family history,' she said. 'I can understand the whole matter is very painful for you, apart from the awkward fact that she seems to have been murdered. I think I'll go to bed now—and thank you again for putting me up.' She went to the door, but just as she reached it, she turned and said with a slight ironic smile, 'This brother of yours, I hope he really exists, my dear. Good night.'

She went out, closing the door behind her.

*

Next morning, when they had had a breakfast of coffee, toast and honey, Margaret said that she would like to see Mrs Digby, to discuss what the two of them were to do in the immediate future. Henrietta pressed her to stay at Curlingham House for as long as it would help her and Margaret thanked her, but with a vagueness which suggested that she was not really considering the offer. However, if she had any other plans she did not say what they were. She telephoned Mrs Digby at her sister's house, then told Henrietta and Patrick that she had arranged to meet her housekeeper there and proposed telephoning for a taxi.

Naturally, Patrick offered to drive her over and at about ten o'clock they left together. Henrietta was aware that although it was Sunday, Patrick would not be coming straight home after he had dropped Margaret, but would go to his lab to attend to an experiment that he was carrying out. It was something, she had gathered, to do with the effect of day length on plant growth and it needed his presence for a time on Sundays as much as on any other day.

When he and Margaret had left, Henrietta began in a dilatory way to stack the dishwasher and tidy the flat. There was still a certain amount of debris from the party to be cleared up and the problem of what to do with the bed in the little spare room in which Margaret had slept. She had not made the bed, and if she was going to return for another night Henrietta supposed that it ought to be done. On the other hand, if Margaret did not intend to return, it would be as easy to strip the bed straightaway and put the sheets in the laundry basket as to leave that to be done later.

On the whole, she thought, it seemed best to make the bed. Anything else would look inhospitable if Margaret should return. She did it, then settled down in the sitting-room with the Sunday paper and what very soon caught her eye, though it was not a very long paragraph and was on an inside page, was an account of a fire in Knotlington, and the discovery of a body in the burnt-out house which had been identified as that of a Mrs Emma Carey, from Aberdeen.

It surprised Henrietta that the identification should apparently have been so positive. If the police had had no more to go on than her recognition of the ring that she had noticed on Emma Carey's hand, they were hardly likely to have given her name to the press. Then she remembered that Patrick had given them his sister-in-law's address, and that would no doubt have led them to make contact with the Aberdeen police, who could have checked on the story that he had told them about his brother and the woman's absence. The brother who Margaret had insinuated might not exist.

Henrietta wondered why Margaret had dropped her remark about that as she was about to go to bed. According to Patrick, when Margaret had gone, she had merely been being bitchy, and the best thing would be not to think about it. Rather unfortunately, so he had said, David did exist, and it did not much matter what she believed about it. The police would no doubt trace him sooner or later and she would learn then that she had made a mistake.

Yet Henrietta found herself feeling uneasy about Margaret's casually dropped remark. At the very least it indicated that in spite of the friendliness of that evening, she did not mean to abandon her continual efforts to get under Patrick's skin, to make him feel the underlying malice in her attitude towards him. And that meant that sooner or later he would have to do something about it, and there was only one thing that he could do, and that was to leave Knotlington.

That thought did not fill Henrietta with any dismay. To return to the green fields and downs and quiet villages of southern England, to settle perhaps in Devon or Somerset, with easy access to the University of, say, Bristol or Exeter, would in its way be very pleasant. But perhaps the move would be in the other direction, to Manchester or Leeds, which she thought of as being probably even grimmer and greyer than Knotlington. And she had made friends in Knotlington, and liked this flat, and disliked the sense of insecurity that she felt when she thought of moving. If she had known for certain that they would move, where they were to go and when it was to happen, she would have accepted it cheerfully, but feeling it merely as something hanging over them, with nothing definite about it, it seemed almost like a threat.

Meanwhile, she thought, she might as well start doing something about lunch. Patrick would come home for it, after he had finished with his work in the lab, instead of eating in the Staff Club, as he usually did on weekdays. She went out to the kitchen and had opened the fridge and was contemplating its contents when the doorbell rang.

She felt sure that it was Detective-Inspector Brightmore, returning with more questions or information, as he had told them the evening before that he probably would, but when she opened the door she found Simon Quinn on the landing. In the way that he had, he was standing as still and as stiffly as if he were at attention.

'Hallo!' he said, sounding somehow surprised. The fact that she looked merely her normal self seemed to be in some way unexpected to him. 'How are you? You'd a rough evening with Franks, hadn't you? Sleep all right?'

He was in his usual jeans and sweater, and his rather long fair hair looked if he had forgotten to comb it that morning. His neat little face was paler than usual, as if he himself had not slept particularly well. 'Patrick in?'

Henrietta answered only his last question. 'No, he's gone to the lab. But come in. He'll be back soon, I think.'

She stood aside for him to enter, and he made one of his swift dives past her into the sitting-room; and then came to an abrupt halt.

'How is Franks?' he asked as Henrietta followed him in. 'Very shattered?'

'I suppose so, though it's hard to tell with her,' Henrietta answered. 'Would you like a drink?'

'If you're going to have one.'

'Sherry, or gin and tonic? I'm afraid that's all we've got to offer, unless you feel like whisky.'

'Sherry, please. But, Henrietta . . .'

'Yes?'

'No, it can wait a minute. But there's something I want to tell you. You and Patrick. Or do I mean there's something I want to ask you? A bit of both, actually. And I'm not sure I ought to be here at all, bothering you, but I've got to talk to somebody and Rachel's busy with Tessa. Anyway, it's not the sort of thing that interests her much.'

'Well, just let me go and get the sherry, then you can tell me what you've got on your mind.' Henrietta went out to the kitchen, returning after a minute or two with the drinks.

As Simon took his glass from her and they both sat down on either side of the gas fire, he gave her a long, intent look in which there was a kind of curiosity, as if he still found it strange that she was as composed as she was.

Then he blurted out, 'Of course, you realize that Franks believes Patrick's committed bigamy.'

'I'm sure she doesn't,' Henrietta answered. 'She isn't such a fool.'

'She's a fool where Patrick's concerned. She's ready to believe anything that would give her some power over him. We needn't pretend, need we, that she isn't in love with him, and that she's desperately hurt because it happens that he's in love with you? People oughtn't to be in love after fifteen years of marriage. The whole department knows about all that. And of course they laugh at her about it, when perhaps they ought to be feeling sorry for her.'

'But as he hasn't committed bigamy, what power does it give her?'

'Oh, none. None at all. But for a little while she thought

it did, and now that this woman's turned up dead in her house, perhaps she's pretty sure of it.'

Henrietta sipped her sherry and looked at him frowningly.

'How d'you know about the woman being found dead in her house?' she asked. 'Have the police been to see you?'

'No, but haven't you seen it in the newspaper today? And it was on the early news.'

'Oh, of course. And they've given her name as Emma Carey, haven't they? Well, the probability is that she was married to Patrick's brother, and why she should have gone to Margaret's house is as much of a mystery to us as it is to you.' She did not feel inclined to tell yet again the story of David's behaviour in Aberdeen, as the dead woman had described it to them.

'Only Franks doesn't believe it's such a mystery, you know,' Simon said. 'I was in the lab for a little while this morning. Everyone's there, awfully excited. And Julie Bishop told me what Franks thinks. She always knows more about that than anyone else and she'd a short talk with her before Franks went off to find some accommodation for herself. Apparently she doesn't mean to go on inflicting herself on you. And Julie told me that Franks knows the woman came to see you yesterday afternoon.'

'Yes, that's true, she did.'

'And she believes that Patrick then took her to Franks's house, but didn't go in with her until after he'd seen Mrs Digby leave, then he got this woman to let him in and immediately knocked her out and locked her in the living-room and went ahead and set the house on fire—'

'Stop, stop!' Henrietta cried as she burst out laughing. 'You're making this up, Simon. It's a wonderful story, but of course you know it's nonsense.'

'*I* know it's nonsense, yes,' he agreed solemnly, 'but does Franks? You see, she knows Patrick knew she'd be coming here from the department, not going home, so he'd plenty of time to get things going safely without her walking in on it.'

'There are several things the matter with that,' Henrietta said. 'First of all, Patrick didn't really expect Margaret to come to our party. She'd accepted our invitation, but neither of us dreamt for a moment she'd really come. We were taken quite by surprise when she did. She just doesn't go to parties. So he wouldn't have felt as safe as all that to commit his murder in her house. Then how did he lay his hands on a supply of petrol all of a sudden? It isn't a thing Margaret would normally keep about the house. She hasn't a car. And we don't keep a spare supply of it ourselves, though you'll just have to take my word for that. And then it happens that Patrick spent the whole afternoon in this flat with me.'

'Can anyone confirm that?'

'Simon!'

He gave an embarrassed laugh. 'I'm sorry, Henrietta, I know this sounds a crazy thing for me to ask you. Of course you don't have to confirm it to me. But you may find the police want you to confirm it if Franks tells them her theory of what happened. The alibis that husbands and wives give one another aren't always believed.'

'I seem to remember having said something of that sort myself yesterday evening,' she said. 'But don't tell me Margaret believes all that nonsense. It seems to me much more likely that it's the product of Julie's imagination. I expect it would give her quite a kick to think she was solving a murder. But I'm afraid she's wrong. I admit it's very difficult to understand what that poor woman, Emma Carey, or Emma Anderson, as I can't help thinking of her, was doing in Margaret's house, and it's also very difficult to understand why anyone set Margaret's house on fire, but you yourself know Patrick had nothing to do with either.'

'Oh yes, I know it, but all the same . . . Look, Henrietta, I'm sorry if I've been giving you the wrong impression. I

only came here to warn you about the sort of hell those two
women, Franks and Julie, are cooking up between them. I
didn't give you the idea I believed any of it, did I? I just
thought Patrick ought to know what's being said about
him. I didn't want to upset you.'

'But what do you really believe yourself, Simon?'

'I wish I knew.' He drew a deep breath and let it out
slowly and Henrietta thought it meant that he was about
to change the subject. But when he went on, though his
tone had altered, becoming almost flippant, he was still on
the subject of the fire. 'It's easy to assume, isn't it, that
that house was burnt down by someone who hated Franks.
She's injured plenty of people in her time, and one of them
might have wanted to take revenge. But suppose it wasn't
like that at all. Suppose it was a friend who did it.'

'A friend? Oh, I see, so that she could get the insurance.'

'I know that sounds crazy. But a funny thing happened
the other day. We all laughed at the time, and I'm sure it
really was just a joke, but if there was someone there who
took it seriously . . . No. I know that's just absurd. It didn't
mean anything.'

'What happened?'

'A number of us were having tea in the afternoon. You
know, we have it in that sort of entrance hall. And Franks
joined us and seemed in a worse mood than usual. Something to do with her house, we gathered. She'd thought
she'd managed to sell it and for a pretty good price to
someone who thought it was a thing of beauty. And the
deal was almost through when the chap discovered that its
being a listed building meant that he couldn't even enlarge
the windows. You know the slits of windows, under those
Gothic arches, that it had. And when he found out that he
couldn't put in two big windows with plate glass which he
thought would be quite appropriate in a Victorian building,
he called the sale off. Franks was pretty bitter about it, and
when she'd told us the story she ended up, saying, "Who

will rid me of this turbulent house?" Of course we laughed, and she laughed too. But then she looked round from one to the other of us, and I swear to you she looked just as if she was trying to find out if anyone there would take the hint.' He paused. 'I told you it was absurd, didn't I? It's just a funny coincidence that someone did the job for her.'

'I hope she has better luck than Henry the Second had with the hint that he dropped. He didn't come out of it very well, though it did land Canterbury with a splendid tourist attraction. But you aren't trying to suggest, are you, that Margaret herself burnt her home down, or arranged with someone to do it for her so that she could collect the insurance and build something a bit more convenient? She's got an alibi, you know. She was in the department when the fire must have got started, then she came straight here with Julie.'

'Yes, I know, but the thing keeps on going round and round in my head.'

Henrietta was beginning to get irritated with him. 'If I were you, Simon, I'd leave the whole thing to the professionals.'

He got to his feet. 'Oh, of course you're right. You're so often right, Henrietta, it's rather formidable. Actually, all I meant to do when I came down was to warn Patrick what Franks and Julie are saying about him. Or anyway, Julie. She said she was quoting Franks, but you may be right that it was Julie's own vivid imagination at work. But I don't like to listen to that sort of thing being said about Patrick. He's done such a hell of a lot for me. If he hadn't got me this grant here I'd probably be out in the streets. Jobs aren't easy to get these days. And there'd have been no Rachel and no Tessa. I never forget that, you know. Well, goodbye now.'

He suddenly swooped on Henrietta, kissed her gently on the cheek, then shot out of the door.

It was about half an hour later that Patrick came home.

Henrietta asked him what he had done with Margaret and he replied that she had found a room in a students' hostel. Seeing the two glasses in the sitting-room, he asked Henrietta with whom she had been drinking and she told him about Simon's visit and all the things that he had said. Patrick fetched a third glass for himself, refilled Henrietta's and filled his own. He sat down in the chair where Simon had been sitting.

'I wonder what he really wanted,' he observed.

'I had a feeling he just wants to be in the thick of things, it's so exciting,' Henrietta said.

'I wish myself I could stop thinking about it,' Patrick said. 'That poor bloody woman. I don't suppose we'll ever know why she went to Margaret's house, but if only we'd tried to keep her here—'

He broke off as the telephone rang.

Henrietta went to answer it. She recited their phone number.

'Henrietta?' a man's voice said.

If she had not known that Patrick was sitting in the room behind her, she would have thought that the voice was his. But she knew at once whose it was, the voices of the two of them being so alike.

'David!' she exclaimed.

He kept his voice low-pitched, as if he were afraid that someone might be listening to him, yet there was a sound of intense excitement in it.

'Is it true,' Henrietta?' he demanded. 'I mean, what's in the paper today. That Emma—I never told you about Emma, did I?—but is it true that she was found burnt to death in a house in Knotlington? It isn't true, is it?'

'We believe it is,' she answered. 'Where are you, David? Where are you speaking from?'

Patrick, who had heard her first exclamation, had come up behind her and reached out and now took the telephone from her.

'David!' he said. 'This is Patrick.' Then after a moment of silence, he put the telephone down. 'He's rung off,' he said. 'So that's that. God knows where he is or whether we're going to hear from him again.'

# Five

They returned to the sitting-room and their glasses of sherry. Patrick looked distraught, with an air of helplessness about him which meant that in a moment he would be demanding that Henrietta should tell him what he ought to do. Not that that guaranteed that he would follow any advice that she might be induced to give. It was probably quite safe for her to give him advice, because in the end he would do what he himself thought best. But it helped him to act as if he were dependent.

As she had expected, once they were settled with their drinks on either side of the gas fire, he said, 'Well, what do we do now?'

The wide-spaced grey eyes in his narrow, bony face had a glowering look of anger in them, almost as if he were ready to accuse Henrietta of having somehow failed him in her moment of conversation with David, which troubled her, even though she knew from long experience that the anger was not in fact directed at her.

She fell back on what she was always liable to say in such situations. 'I don't know what we can do.'

'But we've got to do something,' he said. 'We can't just let that bloody fool go wandering around the country when his wife's been murdered.'

'It really was murder, d'you believe?' she asked.

'What else could it have been? If she really was locked into that room and the house was set on fire, of course it was murder. And d'you realize she may have been dead before the fire started? She may have been killed by a blow on the head, or strangled or something, and been bundled into that room and the window broken to make it look as if she'd been trying to get out that way when the smoke

overcame her. I don't know whether the forensic people
will be able to tell us how she actually died, but that's a
possibility, isn't it?'

'No, because why should the key have been turned on
her if she was dead already? Whether she was alive or
dead, someone thought it was necessary to turn the key.
Why did he almost draw attention to the fact that it was
murder?'

'Hmm. Yes, I see what you mean. But it could have been
just one of the mistakes that murderers are often supposed
to make, couldn't it?'

'Just possibly, I suppose.'

'Meanwhile, what are we going to do about it?'

She thought she knew what he wanted her to say, though
he held back from saying it himself.

'We'll have to tell the police all about David, won't we?'
she said.

'About what a crooked bastard he can be, you mean?'

'Yes, and about that telephone call.'

'I'm afraid you're right, though I wish we hadn't got to.
There's something about telling them things like that about
one's own brother that makes one shrivel up inside.'

'Of course, he may have gone to them himself, now that
he knows from us that the story of Emma's death is true.'

'Not David! He'll try to obliterate every sign of his ever
having had any connection with her.'

'But why? It isn't as if he could possibly have murdered
her himself like that in Margaret's house.'

'Oh, it isn't a thing he'd be rational about. It's just
instinctive—always keep clear of the police. And can we
be certain he didn't murder her? Suppose he knew she was
coming to Knotlington to look for him, and he told her on
the telephone to go to that house. He may actually have
given her that address himself sometime or other and said
she'd always be able to get in touch with him if she went
there. After all, he won't have known that she'd written

two letters to me and got hold of my real address—no, that won't work, will it? I don't see how he could have known that she was coming to Knotlington yesterday. She obviously hadn't been in touch with him. And that leaves us with the puzzle of why she went to the house at all. I've a feeling that's the most important part of the problem.'

'I've got a theory about that,' Henrietta said tentatively.

He raised his eyebrows. 'Yes?'

'D'you remember Emma asked you who your boss was?'

'Yes, and we told her the head of the department was Professor Margaret Franks.'

'And she asked if Margaret might have sent her the anonymous card with your correct address.'

'And I said definitely it wasn't the sort of thing she'd do.'

'And Emma asked if her letters to you could have done you any damage with Margaret.'

'Ah,' he said, 'I think I see what you're getting at. You think Emma may have gone to see Margaret to explain that there'd been a mistake and she wasn't to think I'd been keeping a second wife in Aberdeen.'

'Well, it's possible, isn't it?'

He got up and began to roam about the room. When after a moment he had made no answer, Henrietta repeated, 'It's possible.'

'And quite probable,' he said. 'It's the only explanation anyone's come up with so far of what the woman might have been doing in the house.'

'And are you going to tell the police about David?'

'I want to think about it. Let's have lunch.'

They had some cold ham and salad and coffee. But when they had had it Patrick had still not made up his mind how much he intended to tell the police about his brother. He said he thought that he would go for a walk.

'Feel like coming with me?' he asked.

It seemed to Henrietta a good idea. They both put on their coats and started out together.

There was only one place for them to go, and that was the Botanic Garden. It was the only open green space anywhere near them where they could escape from traffic. Not that there was anything much to see there in February. A little later in the year there would be banks of rhododendrons and azaleas, as well as sweeps of daffodils in the grass and trim rows of early tulips in the flowerbeds. There would be almond trees in blossom, and later there would be flowering cherries, and then the massive chestnuts would come into bloom, and at last, roses. It was not a great botanic garden, but it was a lung in the midst of the crowded brick and stone of human habitation.

At one time Knotlington had been a town of modest distinction. At its centre there were some handsome, even impressive, Georgian buildings. But then came the areas where Victorian taste had prevailed not too attractively, and beyond that the bungalows, the council houses and the factories of modern times. Patrick and Henrietta did not have to discuss where they would go, but as a matter of course, at the bottom of Tenterfield Road, they turned towards the Garden.

They did not talk much as they walked. To be out in the open felt for a little while like escaping from the problem that entirely dominated their thoughts while they remained at home. Henrietta knew that it was no eseape, that they were taking their problem with them, but while she had to exert herself to keep up with Patrick, whose legs were so much longer than hers that he had to make an effort not to keep getting ahead of her, she found that it felt almost as if they had left some of the horror of what had happened the evening before behind them in their flat.

The afternoon was sunny, and even if it was only wintry sunshine, hardly warming the air, there was no wind and the pale blue sky was cloudless. Once they reached the

Garden, feeling warmed by the briskness of their walk to get there along the busy streets, it seemed natural to drop to a stroll along the paved pathways. There were snowdrops already in bloom along their edges and *Iris reticulata*. After all, spring was not far off. It seemed possible to feel a little cheerful.

When they had been younger—students at London University—they had often spent whole days in Kew Gardens, or sometimes gone strolling along the riverbank from Richmond in the direction of Hampton Court. They had met early in what was the first term for both of them and had entered almost at once on a quiet and undemanding friendship. Henrietta had been working for a degree in English Literature, Patrick for one in Biochemistry. It had been her intention to become a teacher, and perhaps, when she was a little older, to see if she could write. In fact, she had never done either. Not long after she and Patrick, maintained by a temporary research grant that Patrick had been awarded, had got married and while she was still quite pleasantly absorbed in the techniques, quite new to her, of housekeeping, she had unexpectedly been offered a job as a librarian in one of the college libraries and had found it interesting.

When Patrick had gone to his first academic post as an assistant lecturer at Reading University, later to be promoted to lecturer, she had been fortunate enough again to find a job in the library there. But in Knotlington she had made no attempt to repeat this. She was not sure why, but it had had something to do with a feeling that she had that if she were working in the University it might somehow help to complicate his situation there, a situation which she had realized very quickly was going to have complications. It had seemed important to her then to do nothing that might interfere with his life in the place. She had become much more domesticated than she ever had been before, and on the whole had enjoyed it.

Looking back, Henrietta was not sure when she had

fallen in love with Patrick. There had not been any special moment when it had happened, but somehow the easy friendship of the first few months that they had known one another had turned into an aching need for him. He had gone away with a few friends for a skiing holiday at Christmas and a kind of panic had taken possession of her that it was not really to Austria that he was going, but home to Kenya, and that he might never return.

She had not yet taken in the degree of hostility that he had felt to his father and that that chapter of his life was closed. Her own father had died when she was fourteen and she had found it difficult to believe that anyone could hate someone who in the normal course of events should be so very dear to him. How far Patrick's background had been from normal was something that she had come to understand only with time. But a week after he had returned from his holiday they had made love for the first time. It had been the first time for both of them. They had been diffident, but deeply loving, and gradually the discoveries of sex had welded them together.

They had not married for two years. They had thought then that perhaps it would be advisable to do so before he went to his post in Reading, and they had also thought that perhaps they would like to have children. But children had not come and it had not really mattered very deeply to either of them. Henrietta had discovered that maternal feeling was not very strong in her. What was important to her was to be needed by the tall, lean, talented young man with the bony features and the unpredictable temper.

To some extent she had never grown accustomed to being needed by anyone. Her mother, as was shown very clearly in her widowhood, was a strong, independent woman who took for granted that Henrietta should need her and who gave her all that she could of love and protection. But that someone else should need her as she had discovered that Patrick did went on filling Henrietta with surprise.

They had been strolling for a little while in the Botanic Garden when Patrick said, 'You know, the time may have come when we should be thinking of moving on from here. If Simon's right that Margaret really believed I might have gone in for bigamy, and possibly set her house on fire, it doesn't look as if I'll ever sort things out with her.'

'Where should we go?' Henrietta asked.

'I haven't really thought about it,' he said. 'Conditions for work have been good here, in spite of Margaret's attempts to make them impossible. And to do her justice, she's never interfered with my work itself, in fact she's always done her best to help me there. It's on the purely personal level that we've had our troubles. But how would you feel about moving?'

'Just tell me when to start packing and I'll get ahead with it,' she replied. 'But the present moment isn't really the time to start thinking about it, is it? Let's decide we'll think about it seriously when we've sorted out the problem of David and that fearful thing that happened yesterday. One shouldn't try to take important decisions at a time like this. Oh look, talk of the devil!'

What she meant was that Neil Robarts and his wife were approaching them on the path along which they were walking, and it was well known that Robarts had set his heart on leaving Knotlington and finding a post in America. They had a little dog with them, an animal that was probably mostly a Cairn terrier, and which trotted ahead of them on a very long lead, looking rather as if it were he who was taking them for a walk. As usual, the tall Lydia Robarts was walking a little behind her short husband, with her customary air of slightly overhanging him. When they noticed the Careys coming towards them they stood still, waiting for them where they were, although their dog made determined efforts to force them on.

'Hallo,' Robarts said as they met, his heavy, pale face with the bushy eyebrows that seemed to protrude above his gold-rimmed glasses showing no expression of any kind. 'Nice afternoon.'

In spite of the fact that as regards the weather, this was true, it seemed a hopelessly inappropriate remark just then. Lydia Robarts said nothing.

'As a matter of fact, we were just talking about you,' Robarts went on.

Henrietta supposed that Lydia did talk when she and her husband were alone together.

'Were you discussing whether I'd set light to Margaret's house?' Patrick asked. 'Not to mention murdering a poor woman in it.'

'Oh, the fire,' Robarts said in a slightly astonished way, as if he did not think it a subject that needed discussion. 'No, I was just saying I wondered if you'd get the second Chair Margaret's trying to get for the department to give it a bit more status. You know about that, of course.'

Patrick shook his head. 'This is the first I've heard of it.'

'Well, I saw her this morning,' Robarts went on, 'and told her I was thinking of taking up an offer Heinzman thinks they're going to make me from Berkeley. I've been working on him while he's been here and he seems quite keen about it, though of course it may come to nothing. It would be as a visiting professor for a year, with the possibility of a permanency. And I discussed the proposition with Margaret, because she'd have to agree to my having that probationary year in case I should want to come back, and she told me not to rush off because she thought she was going to get this second Chair here and that if she did I'd a very good chance of being appointed to it. But I can't say I trust her. I was just saying to Lydia that if there's really this Chair in the offing, you're a much more likely candidate for it than I am.'

'Not if Margaret's given the choice,' Patrick said. 'But I shouldn't take her too seriously about it. It was probably just a dodge to stop you going away.'

'You'd advise me then to take up the American offer, if it comes to anything?' Robarts said.

'I'd do it if someone would make the offer to me,' Patrick replied, 'but don't let that influence you. Our positions here are slightly different.'

'Yes—yes, I see what you mean. By the way, the police have been round to us, asking where we were yesterday afternoon before we went to your party. They actually seem to think that one of our lot could have set Margaret's house on fire. Waste of their time. Would any of us have done such a thing? *All right!*' This was addressed fiercely to the dog, which had grown tired of waiting and was dragging impatiently on its lead. 'We'd better be going. I'll think over what you've said.'

Robarts and Lydia continued on their walk.

Henrietta and Patrick continued on theirs for a little while, then made for home. When they reached it Patrick said suddenly, 'I think I'd like to go to the lab for a little while. D'you mind?'

'Go ahead,' she said.

As he went to the garage to take out their car, she went upstairs to their flat. She wished that she believed in Patrick's desire to move. Just so long as there was no Margaret Franks involved in the new post. Henrietta found that she had grown very tired of resisting her antagonism to Margaret. She wondered if it would have been as difficult if it had been a case of resisting a sexual jealousy of her. That might have been very painful, but it was strange to discover that two people's almost obsessive dislike of one another could be almost equally so.

As she went into the flat the telephone was ringing.

She reached it before whoever it was grew tired of holding on, and said, 'Hallo.'

It was her mother.

'Henrietta, this awful thing that I read in the paper this morning, is it true?' she asked.

'I'm afraid it is,' Henrietta answered.

'That woman, Professor Franks, has had her house set on fire, and they found a dead body in it?'

'Yes.'

'Why didn't you tell me about it?'

It occurred to Henrietta for the first time that that was something that she ought to have done.

'So much has been happening, I just hadn't got around to it,' she said.

'Are you all right?'

'As well as could be expected. But the truth is, Mum, I don't believe it's quite sunk in to me yet. I mean, how awful it is. The woman—well, we think she'd married David. And she'd been to see us only a short time before it happened. That's really all we know at present.'

'Have the police been to see you?'

'Oh yes, we've talked at length.'

'And do they think Patrick's involved in any way?'

'Mum, you know he isn't.'

'Oh, *I* know he isn't, but do they? I've been thinking about that letter you told me about when you were here, and how we laughed about it. But you've nothing serious to worry about, have you?'

Someone had just rung the front doorbell.

'There's someone at the door,' Henrietta said. 'I'd better go and see who it is. It may even be the police. They said they might be back today.'

'But, darling, hold on for a moment. How worried are you?'

'I suppose as worried as I've ever been in my life, but I'll keep you posted with what's happening.'

'Yes, please do that. And let me know if I can help in any way. And give my love to Patrick. Goodbye.'

'Goodbye.'

Henrietta put the telephone down and went to answer the doorbell.

*

It was not the police, it was plump little Julie Bishop. In her flowered blouse and tight, short skirt, with a jacket of fake fur thrown over them, her patterned stockings and her boots, she stood hesitating on the landing with an air of diffidence that was only contradicted by the penetrating stare of her very blue eyes.

'Am I a nuisance?' she asked. 'Are you busy?'

Henrietta was not busy, yet she felt that Julie was certainly a nuisance. She did not want to see anyone just then.

However, she summoned up as friendly an air as she could manage and said, 'Come in.'

It suddenly struck her, as it never had before, that she did not like Julie. But she realized that she was in a mood to dislike almost everyone. People about whom she had never thought much before, who had simply not mattered to her, now seemed to her to have earned her hostility. She had felt it with the Robartses in the Botanic Garden. She had almost felt it towards her mother, as if she believed it was possible that her mother could be harbouring absurd suspicions of Patrick.

'Patrick isn't in, I'm afraid,' she said.

'No, I know, he's in the department.' Julie slipped into the flat with a faint appearance of caution, as if she were not sure what she was getting into. 'But I thought it might help if I had a few words with you.' She dropped her jacket on a chair in the hall. 'Only perhaps you'll think I'm only interfering. I know things are very difficult for you.'

Henrietta thought it was very probable that she would think that Julie was interfering. Indeed, she could not think of anything that might have brought her that did not imply interference of some sort. But she said, 'I don't suppose it's any more difficult than it is for most people, and nothing at all compared with what it is for Margaret and her Mrs Digby. I believe Margaret's found a room in one of the students' hostels.'

They went into the sitting-room and Julie asked if Henrietta would mind if she smoked a cigarette. The main trouble
about that was that the Careys did not possess such a thing
as an ashtray, but Henrietta fetched a saucer from the
kitchen and Julie, sitting down, lit her cigarette, saying, 'I
gave up smoking only a week ago. I've given it up over and
over again. But then something awful seems to happen,
and I feel I simply can't go on without it. But Patrick used
to be quite a heavy smoker, didn't he?'

'Oh yes, a sixty-a-day man,' Henrietta replied. 'But one
day he stopped.'

'However did he manage that?'

'Well, he just stopped.'

'Without any help of any kind? I mean, didn't he take
to eating a lot of sweets or anything?'

'No, and the ironic thing was that for two or three days
I didn't even notice that he wasn't smoking any more. I
was so used to the eternal cigarette in his hand that I'd
quite stopped thinking about it and it just didn't occur to
me that it wasn't there.'

'And how long ago was that?'

'About ten years.'

'Good heavens! Whenever I stop I find I simply have to
eat sweets, and of course, as I've a bit of a weight problem
anyway, that's a rather bad thing. You mean he simply
stopped one day and never smoked again?'

Henrietta was growing impatient. She did not think that
Julie had come just to discuss her smoking or her weight
problems.

'Of course, Patrick's an extraordinary person,' Julie said.

While ready to agree, Henrietta did not feel like replying.

'That's why it's so maddening to hear the sort of thing
that people are saying,' Julie went on. 'Would you believe
it, the Professor herself is convinced that he had some sort
of relationship with that poor woman who died in the fire?
That's really why I came to see you, Henrietta. I thought

you ought to be warned that there's a nasty sort of rumour going around about it.'

'A rumour which you half believe yourself,' Henrietta suggested.

Julie looked shocked. 'How can you say such a thing? Haven't we known each other for years?'

'It's people one's known for years whom one often knows so little about,' Henrietta said. 'But tell me if you at least believe that he's got a brother.'

'A brother?' Julie puffed smoke out before her and thoughtfully watched the cloud disperse. 'Yes, I'm sure I've heard of him, though I can't remember that I ever met him. Does he come into the matter somehow?'

'Almost certainly, though we don't know the whole story. A difficult character. We're fairly sure he married that woman who died in Patrick's name, and that is why she wrote to him at the University, asking for money and threatening him with court action if she didn't get it. A letter which I'm sure you saw.'

'A letter?' Julie looked uncertain. 'Oh, *that* letter. Yes, I remember it now. But it wasn't actually addressed to Patrick, was it? It wasn't correctly addressed to anyone.'

'But someone took the trouble to write to that woman in Aberdeen and give her Patrick's correct title and address. Who do you think that could have been, Julie?'

A very faint flush appeared on Julie's plump cheeks. Her eyes avoided Henrietta's.

'Someone did that? Someone in the department, d'you mean?' she asked.

'That seems probable, doesn't it?' Henrietta said.

'Oh, surely not,' Julie said. 'I mean, anyone who knew Patrick—Patrick and you . . .'

'But I wonder what happened to that letter, Julie.' Henrietta was in a ruthless mood, and had begun to feel sure that it was Julie who had written to the woman in Aberdeen. Her uncharacteristic vagueness helped to betray her. 'Where did it end up? In a waste-paper basket, or in someone's handbag, to be taken home and answered? Do you realize that if someone did that, whatever they believed was the truth about Patrick, they're actually responsible for the woman's death?'

The flush on Julie's cheeks darkened, but her eyes now met Henrietta's with a touch of glittering defiance.

'I don't understand what you mean by that,' she said.

'Only that if Mrs Emma Carey, neé Anderson, had never been told where Patrick lived and how to find him, she'd probably never have come to Knotlington to see us, and she'd be alive and well at home in Scotland. We don't know for sure what took her to Margaret's house after she'd been to us, but it was the anonymous letter she got that brought her here. Is that going to be a pleasant thought to live with, Julie?'

Julie sprang up from her chair. Some ash from her cigarette fell on the carpet.

'I do believe you're accusing me of having answered that letter!' she exclaimed. 'That's just atrocious. It's absolutely untrue.'

Henrietta was suddenly tired of the subject.

'All right, it's untrue. But tell me why you really came to see me, Julie.'

But Julie was not easily appeased. 'It's no good my trying to tell you, if you believe that sort of thing of me. But I can tell you who wrote that letter, if you want me to.'

'You really can?'

'Yes, it was our dear little friend, Simon Quinn.'

Henrietta stared at her. 'I don't believe you for a moment.'

'Oh yes, it was Simon Quinn,' Julie said. 'As a joke, of course. He thought it was a grand joke to pretend he believed Patrick was a bigamist. He's always playing jokes on people. Malicious jokes, most of them, and they can cause terrible trouble. They can have all kinds of consequences, as this letter to the woman in Aberdeen did. And I've heard him say awful things about people. I've heard him say things about Patrick which you wouldn't think possible. And about the Professor, who's done so much for him. You know she wants to get him on to the staff, so that his job will be permanent. And she's been trying to get him to register for a Ph.D. For some reason he doesn't want to, but what does he say? He tells some of us he thinks he's replacing Patrick in her affections.'

'I don't believe you,' Henrietta said.

'Oh, it's true. Ask Dr Robarts. Ask old Mackintosh.'

'Then, as you said, it was just a rather ill-timed joke. But what have you heard him say about Patrick?'

'Oh, I forget just what it was, but it was something pretty spiteful. Something about him exploiting the Professor's feelings for him to get all sorts of advantages in the University.'

'I don't believe you,' Henrietta repeated.

'All right, you don't. You feel so secure in your relationship with him, don't you? But a time may come when you'll have to give it a bit more thought than you've done so far.'

'Julie, why did you really come to see me this afternoon?'

Julie seemed about to make some violent answer, but then she closed her lips firmly. The flush on her face faded.

'I'm sorry, Henrietta, I've been saying all sorts of things I shouldn't have,' she said. 'It was you thinking that I could have written that letter to your sister-in-law, or whatever she was. I didn't know you thought that sort of thing of me. I thought we were quite good friends. I only came to warn you that people are saying things about Patrick which I thought would be a pretty nasty shock for you if you heard them all of a sudden from someone who didn't care how unkind they were being. It might even be the police. I don't know how much they've found out by now, but I can tell you they've been asking several of us questions about Patrick. They've been asking the Professor questions about him. About him and that brother of his. And of course, we've all had to say we know nothing about the brother. Do you really not know where he is, Henrietta, because I think it may be important.'

'All I can tell you about him is that he telephoned us earlier today,' Henrietta replied. 'But when Patrick asked him where he was, he rang off. For all we know, he may even not be in this country. You can't always tell if a telephone call is coming from abroad. On the other hand, he'd seen a report of his wife's death in the newspapers this morning, so he's probably somewhere in England, or possibly Scotland.'

'What about in Knotlington?'

'Even that's possible.'

There was a pause. Julie had stubbed out her cigarette and seemed about to extract another from the packet in her handbag, but then changed her mind, snapped the handbag shut and turned towards the door. Henrietta hoped that she was about to leave, but Julie changed her mind once more and turned back.

'When that woman came to see you . . .' she began hesitantly.

'Yes?' Henrietta said.

'Did she try to get anything out of you? Help of any kind, or, say money?'

'Are you asking if she tried to blackmail us?'

'Well, if by any chance Patrick's brother was in Knotlington, and she turned up here at the same time, it can hardly have been coincidence, can it? And if he's the kind of character you seem to think he is, could they have cooked up something together to get money out of Patrick?'

'And when that didn't work, David lured her to Margaret's house and managed to shut her in somehow and set the place on fire? Aren't we getting into the realm of the absurd?'

'I suppose so. But someone did just that, after all, and

one's always told that most murders are committed within the family. But I must be going. I'm sorry I lost my temper like that a moment ago, but I just can't bear not being believed. I'm funny that way. It's awful to realize one isn't trusted. The Professor trusts me with everything. That's why we get on so well, although we're so different. Luckily I've got all her notes and papers safe in the filing cabinet in my office. It'll help her over the next few weeks, I expect, to be able to get on with her book.'

'You've got *what?*' Henrietta asked.

'The notes she's been collecting over a lifetime. She's got a contract for a book, you know. Getting ahead with it will help take her mind off her trouble over the house.'

'Didn't she keep her notes in the house?'

'Oh, she'd sometimes take odd things home to work on in the evenings, but she'd bring them back next day.'

'Your house is on fire, all your children are gone . . .'

'What?'

'Nothing. Nothing at all. Well, thank you for looking in, Julie. I'm sure you meant it for the best. I'm sorry we quarrelled.'

Julie drew back her lips in a smile that showed her very white teeth.

'Anyway, we've made friends again,' she said. 'Goodbye.'

Henrietta saw her out of the flat and heard her car start down below as she drove away.

Henrietta was glad that she had gone. She did not feel inclined to brood on the things that Julie had told her, but would have liked to put the whole matter out of her mind. Going to the kitchen, she began to consider instead what she should cook for the evening meal which she had never been able to bring herself to call dinner, although for her and Patrick it was the main meal of the day. In the end she decided to warm up something frozen. The local super-market ran a quite good line in chicken and asparagus pies.

She took one out of the freezer and lit the oven, preparatory
to putting the pie into it. She fell back also on frozen peas,
then exerted herself to the extent of peeling some potatoes.
Then she made some batter, thinking that it would not be
too demanding to make some apple fritters. It was about
half past six when she heard Patrick's key in the door.

But he was not alone. Margaret Franks was with him.

She made an apologetic sort of grimace when she met
Henrietta.

'I'm sorry, I'm sure you didn't expect to see me back,'
she said, 'but Patrick persuaded me it would be all right.'

'Of course it is,' Henrietta said. 'Your bed's made, ready
for you.'

'Oh, I'm not staying for the night, though many thanks,'
Margaret replied. 'I've got a room in Bradley Hall. But I
didn't know what to do about dinner. I couldn't face going
into the Staff Club and having everyone looking at me and
probably asking me questions. I was thinking of going to
a restaurant in town when Patrick suggested I should come
home with him.'

'We've enough to eat, have we?' Patrick asked.

'Oh yes, though it won't be very exciting,' Henrietta said.
They went into the sitting-room together. 'How's your Mrs
Digby?'

'Better off than I am, actually,' Margaret said. 'She
can stay with her sister and borrow her sister's clothes. I
shall have to go shopping for some tomorrow and I do
so hate shopping. I used to enjoy it once, but everything
seems to have gone wrong with the shops recently. No one
seems to think, if you're past about thirty, that you may
actually want to buy anything, and so no one pays you any
attention. And if you go to one of the little shops where you
do still get personal attention, the prices are out of this
world.' She was still dressed in the well-cut grey suit in
which she had arrived at the Carey's party the evening
before, the price of which, when it was new, would probably

have seemed out of this world to Henrietta, but just now it was looking a little crumpled and the worse for wear. Margaret was looking a little crumpled and the worse for wear herself. Her light brown curls were uncombed, there were deep shadows under her grey eyes and her lips had a pinched look.

'You'd like a drink,' Patrick stated. 'Whisky?'

'Please.'

He went out to the kitchen to fetch the drinks, and as he returned Henrietta said, 'Julie called in here a little while ago.'

'What did she want?' he asked.

'That's what I couldn't make up my mind about,' she answered. 'I think it was just curiosity, and to discuss how to stop smoking. And to say a few rather malicious things about Simon. I didn't know they didn't like one another.'

'Oh, she's a very curious little animal, that young woman,' Margaret said. 'If I had any secrets I'm sure she'd nose them out in no time. But tell me, have the police been back to see you today?'

Henrietta shook her head. 'They said they might come, but so far they haven't. Do you think that means they've got some lead on what happened in your house yesterday?'

'I don't know of anything, except that they've made a pretty positive identification of the woman who died there,' Margaret said. 'They've been in contact of course with the police in Aberdeen and found she was an Emma Anderson who lived there and who—I'm sorry, Henrietta and Patrick, I know it's very upsetting for you, but she got married recently to someone who was calling himself Patrick Carey—'

She stopped, because the doorbell rang.

'That's probably the police now,' Patrick said.

But again it was not. It was David.

# *Six*

David was an inch or so taller than Patrick and the better looking of the two. Though they were very much alike, with the same thick fair hair and similar narrow faces, David's features were smoother, less pointed, less bony than Patrick's, and his wide-spaced grey eyes usually had an easygoing amiability that Patrick's often lacked. On the other hand, they could express a nervous anxiety, a kind of evasiveness, that was unlike Patrick's direct gaze. He was wearing a short quilted anorak over a dark suit.

Henrietta's exclamation of, 'David!' brought Patrick quickly to the hall. He grasped David's arm and drew him hurriedly inside, as if he felt that he might turn and run if he did not secure him.

'Sorry. I know you weren't expecting me,' David said a little breathlessly, 'but is it all right—my coming like this, I mean?'

Patrick closed the door behind him.

'You must know we've been hoping you'd show up,' he said. 'We didn't altogether expect it, after the way you rang off yesterday. We thought you'd try to keep out of the whole affair.'

'That's what I thought I'd do at first,' David said. 'But for various reasons I had second thoughts. I hope you're alone.'

'As it happens, we've a visitor,' Patrick said. 'You'd better come in and meet her.'

David turned quickly to the door.

'No, I'll come back another time, when you're on your own.'

Patrick grabbed him by the arm again.

'No, now you're here, you'll stay. We've a lot to talk
about.'

'But I'll come back, Patrick, I really will, when you're
free.'

'I don't think we'll rely on that. Come on in.' Patrick
took David's anorak from him, and led him firmly into the
sitting-room.

It worried Henrietta that about the first thought she had
had when she saw David had been that although the meal
she had prepared could be stretched to feed three people,
she could not think how she could make it enough for four.
That surely was not the kind of thing that she should
immediately have considered on seeing before her the husband of a woman who had been very fiendishly murdered,
a man, moreover, who might somehow be concerned in her
death. That did not seem impossible. Her mind, Henrietta
thought, had really been becoming almost dangerously con-
ditioned by the continual planning and organizing that goes
with a domestic life if such a thought could immediately
dominate it.

They found Margaret standing with her back to the fire.
Patrick drew David into the room. She gave him a long,
steady look, to which he responded with an air of uneasy
embarrassment.

Patrick said, 'My brother David, Margaret. David, this
is Professor Franks, whose house, I believe you know, was
burnt down.'

'Your brother?' Margaret said. Something sardonic had
entered her gaze. 'I believe I owe you an apology, Patrick,
for something I said last night when you and Henrietta
were being so kind to me.'

'That my brother perhaps didn't exist?' Patrick said.
'Well, here he is in the flesh, though we don't know any
more than you do where he's come from. A drink, David?'

'Thank you,' David said.

'Whisky? Sherry? Gin and tonic?'

'Gin and tonic, please, with ice, if you've got it. But not too strong. You've a way of making them pretty strong, I seem to remember. And I want to keep my head.' He did not look at Patrick as he said it. He was returning Margaret's gaze with a look of increasing self-confidence. He knew that he was an attractive man who could usually charm people when he chose and he seemed to have sized Margaret up very quickly as a woman who would not be unresponsive to him. 'I must tell you how much I sympathize with you for your loss, Professor.'

'Isn't your loss of rather more consequence?' she inquired.

'My loss? Oh, you mean the tragedy of the death of that poor woman who was in the house. Yes, that was terrible, wasn't it? But I don't believe in the identification of her, you know. It doesn't seem possible. It's true I've tried to get in touch with Emma in Aberdeen and have been told she's gone away, but it doesn't make sense that she should be in your house, does it? Can't you think of anyone else it could have been?'

'David, do you seriously mean that dead woman wasn't Emma?' Henrietta asked. She knew that he would lie about the matter if that seemed to him advisable, but if he was lying at the moment his callousness was even more than she would have expected of him.

'Well, can you tell me anything that could have taken her to Professor Franks's house?' he said. 'I've been thinking about that all day, ever since I saw the item in the newspaper, and particularly since I couldn't get in touch with her by telephone, and the only conclusion I've arrived at is that it wasn't Emma. How can they have made an identification of her so soon?'

Patrick had just returned from the kitchen to which he had gone to fetch the drink for David.

'She was wearing a ring, two opals with an emerald between them, which Henrietta recognized as hers,' he said.

'A ring which Henrietta recognized—?' For the first time David sounded shaken. 'You saw her, then?'

'She called on us yesterday afternoon,' Patrick answered.

'Even so . . .' David began, then stopped, his forehead wrinkling. 'No, even if she came here, a thing like a ring isn't enough for them to go on.'

'No, but when Henrietta identified it,' Patrick said, 'it gave the police an idea where to look, and we could give them Emma's address as I'd had a letter from her on Friday morning. The Aberdeen police did the rest.'

'Mr Carey, do I understand that you haven't been living in Aberdeen yourself?' Margaret asked.

Since she had seen the first letter from Emma Anderson, or Emma Carey, wrongly addressed but reaching Patrick in her department, there was something distinctly devious in her asking the question.

'No, I've been away for some time—in London,' David answered in a hurried way. 'She was to have followed me as soon as I'd got settled. And that's probably where she is now, looking for me. She probably got tired of living alone. There was no reason on earth why she should have come to Knotlington.'

'And when did you get to Knotlington yourself?' Margaret asked.

'I've just driven up,' he answered.

'You came by car?'

'Yes.'

'And you came here because of what you read in the papers this morning?'

Margaret had adopted the authoritative, inquisitorial air that she might have used if she had been conducting the examination of a student. She gave no sign that David's charm had made any impression on her.

As if he realized this, he shed a good deal of it. Abruptly he said, 'Isn't that what I said? You don't suppose I'd simply have remained in London after I'd read about it.

And you haven't answered my questions, Professor. Can you think of anything that could have taken her to your house, and can't you think of anyone else it might have been?'

'The answer to both questions is no,' Margaret said. She turned to Patrick. 'I think, Patrick, it might be best if I didn't stay to dinner. You and your brother must have a great deal to talk about which you'd sooner do without a visitor being present. If you'll phone for a taxi, I'll have dinner in town.'

Patrick began to say that there was no reason at all why she should leave, and then when she insisted that it would be best for her to do so, he offered to drive her to a restaurant himself, but she refused his help.

'No, a taxi, please,' she said. 'Am I right that you and your brother haven't seen each other for some time? I don't want to intrude on your meeting, and I don't think he'll talk much while I'm here.'

So a taxi was ordered, while Henrietta reflected that after all there would only be three people to feed and that that could be managed.

While they were waiting for the taxi, Margaret again addressed David.

'Do I understand that you haven't been to the police yet to tell them what you know of your wife's movements?'

'Didn't I explain I know nothing about her movements?' he said sullenly. 'Patrick and Henrietta know more about them than I do, if she came to see them. I can understand she might want to visit them, but why she went on to you is beyond me.'

'So you haven't been to the police yet.'

'No.'

'But of course you're going.'

'That's something I'll discuss with Patrick. I don't know yet what he's been telling them.'

'I see.'

Just what she saw she did not make clear, and only a few minutes later the taxi arrived and Margaret, after making an ambiguous remark that it had been very interesting to meet David, left for the restaurant of her choice. Patrick saw her down to the taxi, then returned to the flat, shut the door of it with a slight slam and came into the sitting-room. He picked up his glass and drained it.

'Now then,' he said, 'let's have a little truth. We can do without the lies. When did you get to Knotlington?'

David gave a slight groan and dropped into a chair. He took his head in his hands.

'All right, all right, I'll tell you everything,' he said, 'but I didn't see why I should while that woman was there. I got to Knotlington yesterday.'

'What brought you?'

'I should have thought you could have worked that out for yourself. I knew Emma was coming.'

'How did you know that? Had you been in touch with her?'

'No, and that's how I guessed where she probably was. Besides that, she happens to share a flat in Aberdeen with a friend, and I'd got the friend on the telephone, and she'd told me Emma had just left to join her husband. I hadn't mentioned that it was her husband ringing up, you see, and I knew the friend believed her husband lived in Knotlington, so I got up here as quickly as I could, hoping I'd be able to see you to explain things before she got here. But I was too late. I drove up here just behind a taxi, and when the taxi stopped here I saw Emma get out. So I didn't see any point in coming to see you just then and I drove down to the bottom of Tenterfield Road and waited there. I didn't know, of course, how long I might have to wait, but in fact, it wasn't very long, and when she came it was on foot and I saw her get on to a bus that took her into town. I followed the bus and saw her get out at a stop outside a hotel called the Riverdale. So I managed to park my car and went into the hotel too, but by then she'd vanished, so I asked them if Mrs Patrick Carey had come in yet, as if we'd had an appointment to meet there, and they told me she had only stayed long enough to look a number up in a telephone directory and try to make a phone call, then had gone straight out again. And that's all I know. God's truth, Patrick, that's all I know, and it seems to me I'm talking a hell of a lot too much. Can't you do a little?'

'You didn't see her go to Margaret Franks's house?' Patrick asked.

'No, how could I? I dare say it was her address Emma was looking up, and probably her whom she tried to call, and she may have gone straight to the house, for all I know, but how was I to guess that? I booked in the hotel myself, thinking I'd get hold of her later in the evening, then I just waited. But of course, she didn't come.'

'So you *do* believe the woman who died in the fire was Emma?'

Perhaps it was the sternness in Patrick's voice that affected David, but his face suddenly crumpled, and tears began to pour out of his eyes. He looked remarkably young, almost childish. With his voice shaking, he cried, 'Of course it was! It must have been! But I wasn't going to admit it to that arrogant bitch you'd got here, who probably knows all about Emma's death, what she was doing in the house and who set the place on fire. She may have done it herself, for all I know.'

'She's got an alibi.' There was no sympathy in Patrick's tone as he went on, 'And you can dry up the crocodile tears, David. Your love for Emma doesn't seem to have been very profound. Why didn't you get in touch with us yesterday evening when Emma didn't come back to the hotel?'

With the tears still on his cheeks, David answered, 'I tried to.'

'You did?'

'Yes, I rang your number, but there wasn't any answer. Anyway, I wasn't sure that I wanted to see you. It was Emma I wanted.'

'What time was that?'

'Oh, about half past six, quarter to seven, some time like that.'

Henrietta said, 'That's when we'd all have left to go to the fire. The flat would have been empty.'

'Well, there was no answer,' David said again. 'So I thought after a bit I'd come and see you. I started to drive up here, then I ran into a fearful crowd, traffic was being diverted, there was a mass of people in the street, and I could see that there was a fire ahead. So I parked my car and got out to have a look at what was happening, and when I got to the spot where the police were keeping people back, I saw you, Patrick, standing talking to a tall bloke who was obviously a policeman, and there was a woman there with you, the same one who's just been here, though of course I didn't know who she was, but plainly you were pretty involved and I didn't think it was much use hanging around, trying to get hold of you. So I went back to the hotel, and the hotel people will tell you that's what I did.'

'And you rang up this morning to ask if what you'd read in the newspaper was true,' Patrick said, 'but you rang off the moment I spoke to you. Why was that?'

'Oh, don't you understand?' There was almost a wail in David's voice as he spoke. 'I wanted to know if it was true that Emma was the woman they'd found dead in the house, and Henrietta had told me it was, but I didn't want to get involved in a lot of explanations of what I was doing here. I wasn't even sure, if it really was Emma, if I was going to stay in Knotlington or go straight back to London. I had to think.'

'And when you'd done enough thinking, you decided after all to come and see us. Why was that?'

David brushed the tears away from his cheeks with the back of his hand. Henrietta remembered that he had always cried very easily. In the days when Patrick had still been trying to induce him to see a psychiatrist who conceivably might cure him of the habit of lying, he had often managed to check the pressure that Patrick was putting on him by pathetic weeping.

'I thought after all I'd like to talk to you,' he said. 'I thought you might be able to give me some advice.'

'All right, I will,' Patrick said. 'Go to the police.'

'I can't do that.'

'Why not? You say the hotel people will give you an alibi.'

'Well, I suppose they would, but you can't always trust people, can you?' Coming from the most untrustworthy person whom she personally had ever known, Henrietta found a certain charm in this statement of David's. He went on, 'I'd have to explain what I'd been doing in Scotland, and how I knew Emma, and all that, and it might be awkward.'

'What were you doing in Scotland?' Patrick asked. 'Hiding out?'

A rather stubborn look appeared on David's face, as if he did not intend to admit too much. 'You might call it that, though I'd say it was an exaggeration. Anyway, there were some people in London I wanted to avoid.'

'What had you been doing in London?'

'If I tell you, you'll only despise me.'

'It could be I do that already.'

'And haven't you always shown that!' Anger flared for a moment in David's reddened eyes. 'A brainy chap like you, with a nice steady job, and a nice wife and a nice flat, and a nice pension waiting for you some day. Of course you despise me.'

'Wasn't Emma a nice enough wife for you?'

'Oh, she was, she was, that's a part of what made it so awful. But she was bound to find me out sometime. I mean, that I wasn't a professor and hadn't a steady job of any kind, or any house to offer her, and I couldn't face that. I just had to get out. It was the only thing to do.'

'You still haven't told me what you were doing in London.'

'Well, for some months I'd been working as barman in a pub called the Holly Tree in the Earls Court district. Not the kind of pub you'd ever think of going into, though my boss wasn't a bad chap in his way, and some of the regulars were interesting. And I was pretty good at the job. I'd done much the same sort of thing in pubs around the country and got a good deal of experience. But the Holly Tree got raided once or twice because there was a suspicion around that they were pushing drugs, and I began to feel it was a place to get away from.'

'And were they pushing drugs?' Patrick asked.

'Oh, good Lord, yes,' David answered casually, 'and I didn't fancy the idea of being caught myself. Anyway, I was getting fed up with the work too. So one night I helped myself to what there was in the till and took off. There were just a few hundred pounds there. And I felt pretty safe they wouldn't look too hard for me if I kept well out of their way, because they couldn't afford to have the police nosing around their affairs. So I thought I'd see what Scotland was like. I'd never been there. And I don't know why I settled on Aberdeen, but anyway I did, and got a cheap room, and a few days after I got there I met Emma in a pub and we took to each other right away.'

'And you told her you were a certain Professor Carey.'

'Yes, it was the first name that came into my head.'

'Have you used it on any other occasions?'

'Oh, once or twice. Not very often.'

'And did it mean anything to Emma, your being a professor?'

'Of course it did. I don't know if she'd have let me move in with her or her friend if she'd thought I wasn't something fairly respectable. And being a professor was a good sort of job to have because she could understand it wasn't a nine to five sort of thing and so while she was out at her work I could hang around, or go wandering about, sightseeing, or anything else I felt like doing. I was pretty much in need of a rest actually, and it gave me some time to think. I didn't want to spend the rest of my life as a barman. It's very hard work, for one thing, even if you get in with people who aren't crooked.'

'But why did you have to marry Emma?'

David made a gesture, spreading out his hands as if he were showing that he had no very good explanation to make.

'She seemed to want it,' he said, 'and I couldn't see anything special against it.'

'Since you didn't mean to stay with her anyway.'

'I hadn't made up my mind about that. As a matter of fact, I rather liked being married to her. It had a peaceful sort of feeling.'

'Then why didn't you stick to her and tell her the truth?'

'The truth! Of God, Patrick, you speak as if it's quite easy to do that! Don't you see the fix I was in? I'd told her I was you before I'd ever thought she and I might settle down together, and that I'd married her in your name, and d'you know, I'm not even sure if that means it was a legal marriage? I believe it was, but I'm not quite certain about it. Then the time was going to come when she'd expect me to leave for Knotlington and of course I couldn't bring her here and I was going to have to confess what I'd done. And I couldn't face doing that. All the same, I wasn't meaning to desert her. What I thought I'd do was just take off for the South and look for a job and when I'd found

something decent I'd get in touch with her again and tell
her this truth you're so keen on, and if she cared for me
still, she would have joined me. But I couldn't find the sort
of job I was looking for. It wasn't because I was being
ambitious, it's just that there aren't any jobs going at the
moment. I was managing by doing a few odd jobs, window-
cleaning, a bit of gardening, repairing things for people.
I'm a pretty good handyman, and you can ask people a
hell of a lot for the small sort of jobs they can't get a real
professional to do, and of course all the payments are in
cash, so there's no question of income tax, and I was getting
unemployment benefit. But then something rather awkward happened.'

'It didn't have anything to do with some letters you
wanted her to post for you, did it?' Patrick asked.

'Oh, she told you about that, did she? Clever of you to
guess it. Yes, it did. I'd had an idea, you see, something
I'd picked up in a paper I read one day, and I thought it
was pretty neat. Those letters were all applications for jobs
I'd seen advertised, good jobs, and all just a little way out
of London. And I wanted her to post them in Aberdeen,
getting them an Aberdeen postmark, then I was going off
to London and was going to let her know where I was
staying, so that if any answers came she could let me know,
and I'd be able to go to be interviewed, saying I'd come
from Aberdeen and getting my expenses paid for a journey
from Scotland, when all I'd done was travel from London.
It would have been quite profitable. I'd kept my old car,
you see, that I'd had when I was a barman and making
fairly good money, and could have done the short journey
very cheaply. But I hadn't thought it out. I'd forgotten that
for the scheme to work I'd have to let her know where I
was staying, so that she could let me know if I got any
answers to my applications. And I didn't make up my mind
till yesterday whether or not I should do that. And then
suddenly I thought I would, I'm not sure why. I wanted

to see her again, I suppose. I was missing her more than I'd expected. So I telephoned to ask if there'd ever been any answers, and to say I was in London and to tell her some story of why I'd been delayed there, and I got that reply I told you about from her friend that she'd gone off to join her husband, and so I knew she'd be coming here. And I took off as fast as I could, hoping I could get to you before she did, and I've told you the rest. And you needn't say I've been a fool, because of course I know it.'

'Fool is a bit of an understatement,' Patrick said. He was watching his brother with a troubled look in which there was something that was almost admiring, as well as a degree of affection. He went on, 'But there's nothing for it now, you know, David, you'll have to tell this story to the police. You might perhaps omit the bit about the letters. It doesn't seem very important. But you'll have to tell them the rest.'

'What, tell them I was pushing drugs, that I nicked that money from the till, that I got married on false pretences —are you mad?' David asked explosively.

'Wouldn't that be better than being arrested for arson and murder?' The look of kindness on Patrick's face had gone. There was repulsion there now, and contempt. 'If you don't ring them now, I'm going to.'

'No!' David sprang to his feet. 'I didn't set the house on fire and I didn't kill Emma and I'm not going to grovel to the police, trying to persuade them I didn't.'

'No one else that we know of had the faintest motive for killing Emma,' Patrick said. 'No one else had even seen her before.'

'And you believe I'm a murderer!'

'I didn't say that.'

'But it's what you believe. And I'm not staying here to have an accusation like that made against me. I'm leaving now.'

'Wait a moment, David—'

'No!'

David made a dive for the door. Grabbing him by the arm, Patrick tried to hold him back, but besides being the taller of the two brothers, David was a good deal the stronger, as well as being filled with a sudden frenzied rage and fear that gave a fierce increase of power to his movements. He shook Patrick off, and rushed out of the room and out of the door of the flat and down the stairs. Patrick and Henrietta heard his car start down below.

They looked at one another helplessly for a moment, then Patrick picked the telephone up and began to dial 999. But before he had finished dialling he quietly put the telephone down again.

'Let's eat,' he said.

For only two people after all, there was more than enough. Henrietta did not bother with the apple fritters, but opened a tin of fruit salad. They ate almost in silence, each apparently concentrating on the act of eating, though the probability was that neither of them could have said afterwards what they had eaten.

But after a time Patrick said, 'All right, what ought I to have done?'

They were sitting at the dining-table in the kitchen, and had started drinking coffee.

'As if I could tell you!' Henrietta answered. 'He's your brother.'

'That's the hell of it,' Patrick said. 'He is. And I've always had a faint, guilty sort of feeling that it's partly my fault that he is what he is.'

'That's nonsense.'

'Is it? I'm five years older than he is. I was an adolescent, almost grown up, when our mother died. I'd had her love and her gentleness right through my whole childhood, but he lost it when he'd hardly begun to think about anything. And I escaped the moment I could, leaving him to the mercies of that terrible old man in Kenya. I didn't worry about David or what would become of him. And now, every time I see him, I get a feeling that I've failed badly in some kind of duty.'

'That simply isn't true. I wouldn't be surprised if he was already lying his way out of any trouble that came along even while your mother was still alive. All the same, I know what you mean, perhaps because I was an only child and used to long desperately for a younger brother or sister to look after. For some reason, I never wanted an older one. I suppose I wanted to feel sure that I'd always be boss. But what are you going to do now, Patrick? Are you going to phone the police?'

'I suppose I'll have to. Do you think I should?'

'I suppose so.'

'All right, I'll do it now.'

He stood up, but as he did so the doorbell rang.

This time it was the police. Detective-Inspector Bright-more and Detective-Sergeant Dance stood on the landing. They said good evening politely as Patrick took the two big men into the sitting-room, with Henrietta following them.

'Sorry to disturb you,' the Inspector said, 'but we had a phone call just a little while ago from Professor Franks and she told us your brother was with you. We rather want to talk to him.' He looked past Henrietta, through the open door of the room, and added, 'He's gone, has he?'

'So she told you, did she?' Patrick said. 'Yes, he's gone. And I did what I could to persuade him to get in touch with you, but I'm afraid I failed.'

'It didn't occur to you to get in touch with us yourself,' Brightmore said. It was not a question, but a statement; but his tone was not stern, it was merely expressionless. His small, deep-set dark eyes held a look of cool detachment which Henrietta found more frightening than anything more obviously threatening would have been. 'How long ago did he leave?'

'I should think about half an hour,' Patrick answered.
'Do you know where he's gone?'

'No. He told us he'd booked in at the Riverdale Hotel,
but I'd be a little surprised if you find him there.'

'You know why we want to see him, of course.'

'To see if he can identify the dead body of the woman in
that house as his wife, I suppose.'

'It's a bit more than that. Actually, I don't think he'll
be able to identify her, just by looking at what's left of her.
That'll have to be formally arranged, but she was wearing
a small denture which the fire didn't destroy, and we've
already had confirmation from her dentist in Aberdeen that
it was one he made for her. No, what we'd like to know a
bit about is the curious fact that he appears to have married
her in your name. So Professor Franks told us. Does that
mean anything to you?'

'Yes, of course it does. And I realize I've got to tell you
the whole story. So sit down and I'll get going.'

'Would you like some coffee?' Henrietta asked. 'I'd just
made it when you came.'

'Thank you, that would be very acceptable,' Brightmore
replied.

She went out to the kitchen, and put the coffee pot and
some cups on a tray. She was boiling inside with anger with
Margaret Franks. She had often been angry with her, but
never quite as fiercely as she was at the moment. She felt
that what she had done was a betrayal of Patrick, not
because in the end he would not have made the call to the
police himself, but because it had been a sign of distrust,
as well as an assertion of her right to interfere in his
actions.

Returning to the sitting-room, Henrietta found the men
sitting down, though they got to their feet when she entered,
then sat down once more as she handed round the coffee.

'And now I'll try to tell you everything we've learnt about
my brother,' Patrick said, 'but please remember I don't

guarantee it as the truth. It's what he's told us, but from childhood he's had a remarkable gift for fantasy. He's what's generally called a pathological liar. That's to say, I honestly believe he can't help it. But some of it may be true.'

The Inspector put two teaspoons of sugar into his coffee, and the Sergeant three.

'Go ahead,' the Inspector said.

Patrick went ahead. He told the two detectives almost everything that David had told him and Henrietta, but not quite all. He skated over David's account of why he had suddenly left London and gone to Aberdeen. He said nothing about drug-pushing, or money stolen from the till in a public house. He only said vaguely that he believed his brother had got into trouble of some sort in London and had chosen to disappear for a while. He said nothing about David's unsuccessful attempt at fraud, obtaining expenses for his travelling when he applied for jobs. But he gave a fairly full account of David's relationship with Emma, as David himself had told it, of the letters to himself that apparently had caused all that had happened since, and of what David had done on coming to Knotlington.

At the end of it, Brightmore nodded thoughtfully. 'And that leaves us no nearer knowing what Mrs Emma Carey was doing in Professor Franks's house. As you've told us the story, your brother himself didn't know. But it still looks as if he's the only person who was here last night who had any relationship with her at all—apart from yourself, that is, and we aren't taking that into account.'

'It's all right, Inspector. I know you are taking it into account,' Patrick said. 'I certainly should in your place.'

A bleak little smile twitched at the detective's thin lips.

'I don't think you need feel uneasy,' he said, 'though as a matter of fact, something else has come up about which we'd like to ask you a question or two. We've had another telephone call at the station, not from Professor Franks, at

least the man who took the call is almost certain it was a
man who was calling. An anonymous call. And all the caller
said was, 'Look for the key to Professor Franks's house in
Dr Carey's flat.' He just said that and rang off. Now, at a
time like this we're accustomed to getting a number of
anonymous calls, and we don't take much notice of them.
What satisfaction the callers get from making them I don't
pretend to understand. But in among the hoax calls and
the deliberately misleading ones there's sometimes one that
has a grain of truth in it, and we've got to do our best to
investigate—'

'It's all right, Inspector,' Patrick said once more, inter-
rupting Brightmore's careful introduction to what he
intended to say. 'You want to know if we know anything
about the key that let someone into Professor Franks's
house to set it on fire, and you'd like to have a look round.
You haven't a search warrant, I imagine, but you'd like to
see if we'll be cooperative and let you look. Well, go ahead.
Any objections, Henrietta?'

She shook her head.

'But a key's a very small thing,' she said. 'Even if we'd
got it, I'm sure we could have found a dozen places here
where it could be lost to sight for good. But do go ahead.
We'll even help you. If anyone brought it here, it's probably
in this room, because it's the only place, apart from the
room where Professor Franks slept last night, where anyone
but ourselves has been. And I don't suppose you're interested in Professor Franks's room, because she's hardly likely
to have hidden her key there, then rung you up in a mascu-
line voice and told you where to look for it. It's true she's
got a deep voice, which might sound like a man's on the
telephone . . .' She had begun to wander about the room,
making a show of looking inside the odd ornamental vases
and bowls on the mantelshelf as if she were searching for
the key, but suddenly she broke off. 'Oh, look at this!' she
exclaimed.

She picked something out of a little old Chelsea bowl that stood on top of a bookcase and held it up.

'Put that down!' the Inspector barked at her and sprang forward. 'Don't touch it any more!'

'But it's a key,' she said. 'A Yale key. And I know Margaret Franks's key was a Yale, but we've a different kind of lock. It can't be ours.'

'And now it's got your fingerprints on it,' he said, losing his air of detachment for the first time since they had met him. 'Just put it down where you found it, Mrs Carey, and we'll take it and the bowl away with us, if you don't mind. And we'll ask you to call in at the station to have your prints taken, so that we can see if there are any on it other than yours. My guess is there won't be.'

'But I didn't use it to get into her house and set it on fire,' Henrietta protested. She had quickly dropped the key back into the bowl. 'I've never seen it before.'

'I'm prepared to believe you,' he said, 'but we've got to be able to eliminate the prints you've just made in case there are others. But as I said, my guess is that we'll find the key was wiped clean before it was left here. That's not something we can take for granted, however. We'll have to take the bowl and the key away with us now, and ask you to come down to the station so that we can take your prints.'

'You'll find Mrs Forbes's on the bowl,' Henrietta said. 'She's our cleaning lady, and she's a great one for dusting all these odds and ends here.'

'Then we may have to get her prints as well,' Brightmore said. 'And probably those of all the people who've been in this room since yesterday evening. Can you give me a list of everyone who's been here? It would save time if you can do it now.'

Henrietta and Patrick exchanged glances, then she began to recite the names of the people who had come to their party on the Saturday evening. He prompted her once or twice, while Sergeant Dance wrote down the names in a notebook that he produced from a pocket. He also produced a plastic bag in which, with his hands wrapped up in his handkerchief so that his own fingers should not touch bowl or key, he stowed them both.

'But of course, we're forgetting someone,' Patrick said. 'My brother David. Till you know if he really went to the Riverdale and is still there, you won't be able to get his prints.'

'Is there nothing he touched while he was here, a glass, perhaps, or a cup?' Brightmore asked. 'Something you're sure will have his prints on it, but probably no one else's, except for your own?'

Henrietta felt a strong inclination to say that there was not, though the glass from which David had drunk while he had been in the flat was still unwashed. But she left it to Patrick to answer as he chose, and after a moment's hesitation, he said, 'Yes, there's a glass. But he didn't plant that key here, or make you an anonymous call. I'm prepared to swear to that.'

'If you'd get us the glass . . .'

Patrick nodded and left the room. When he returned, holding the glass in a tea-towel, Sergeant Dance produced another plastic bag in which to carry it. The Inspector thanked Patrick, and the two men then took their leave, Brightmore repeating that the sooner they came to the station to have their fingerprints taken, the more convenient it would be for everyone, including themselves.

'We'll come right away,' Patrick said.

Yet as the detectives left, he lingered, then suddenly put his arms round Henrietta and held her close.

'Arson and murder,' he said. 'What's their next move going to be? Because of course they haven't given up the idea that I may be the guilty man they're looking for. Our hiding that key here for them to find could be just a very clever dodge, couldn't it? Would we ever have done it if I were really a murderer? Of course not. And that makes it so likely that it's just what we really did. And rung them up to tell them where to look, and you immediately finding the key—oh, it all fits. It strikes me, we're a pair of very clever criminals, my darling. But a little too clever for our own good. Now let's get going.'

# Seven

That night, in the darkness, lying side by side in bed, neither Henrietta nor Patrick could sleep. For a time, after they had switched their light off, each had stayed very still, afraid of disturbing the other, but something in that very stillness and in the sound of the other's breathing had told them both that sleep for the present was not coming to either. Their trip to the police station had had no results. There had been no fingerprints but Henrietta's on the Yale key that she had found in the Chelsea bowl, and the few that were on the bowl itself, it was almost certain, would turn out to be Mrs Forbes's. The whole event had had a kind of dullness, a sense of anti-climax.

That the police had only expected what they had found did not in any way bring reassurance. Someone, it seemed, had acquired the key, used it to enter Margaret Franks's house, had later wiped it clean of fingerprints, then dropped it in the bowl in the Careys' sitting-room and then telephoned the police to tell them where to look for it. Whoever that had been, it had been someone who had been at their party on Saturday evening, and so was someone with whom they had reasonably friendly relations, or it just possibly could have been David. But it was not characteristic of David. If he had dropped the key in the bowl it would simply have been to hide it. He would never have thought of making a telephone call to the police to tell them where it was. The police at all times, he considered, were people best avoided.

After a time a little sigh escaped Henrietta and she stretched a little in the bed. When she did it, Patrick's arm slid out round her neck and lay gently on her shoulder.

'That woman,' he said, 'that Julie—why did she really come to see you?'

'Is that what you've been thinking about all this while?' Henrietta asked.

'Well, it puzzles me,' he said. 'When Margaret was here you obviously didn't want to tell us why Julie had really come. You said something about curiosity having brought her and wanting to stop smoking, which of course was nonsense. But I've been wondering if you yourself have any idea why she came.'

'A hazy sort of idea, and I may be quite wrong. I think curiosity did come into it. She'd have liked to find out a little about David. But also I think she wanted to plant the belief in my brain that it was Simon who wrote the card to Emma, giving her your real address.'

'Simon?' Patrick said incredulously. 'Of all the unlikely people!'

'Oh, she said he did it as a joke. But she also said he'd been making malicious remarks about you, talking about his replacing you in Margaret's affections. As she said, if I didn't believe her I should ask Robarts or Mackintosh. But of course by then I'd made her really angry by practically accusing her of having written to Emma herself.'

'And is that what you think?' Patrick asked. 'That Julie sent that anonymous card to Emma?'

'I wasn't sure if I did or not when I accused her of it,' Henrietta said. 'But the way she reacted more or less convinced me. Her face flushed and she got very angry and she started telling me that the police had been asking questions about you, and then all of a sudden she seemed to want to make peace and patch up our quarrel, and said she'd only been telling me what she had because she thought someone ought to warn me about what was being said. But that only happened when I kept on at her about why she'd really come to see me.'

'Suppose that was the reason why she came,' Patrick

said. 'I mean, to warn you that I'm not beloved by everyone
in the department. You know, one of Margaret's tricks is
that she's got a strange knack of making trouble between
other people. I don't know what satisfaction she gets from
it, unless it's a sort of sense of power. Power to destroy
anything that might look like turning into friendship
between other people in which she wasn't actually included,
or perhaps a kind of revenge because she knows she isn't
beloved herself.'

'Julie told me something very strange about her. I didn't
know what to make of it.'

'What was it?'

'That Margaret didn't keep her notes and papers for her
book in her house, but in the department.'

'But she told us she kept them in the house.'

'That's just it. She said that thing about, "Your house
is on fire, all your children are gone . . ." and then she said
that her papers were the only children she'd ever have and
that years of work had gone up in flames and that she'd
never write her book now.'

'And what d'you think that means?'

She did not answer at once, but moved closer to him,
resting against the warmth of his body.

'If Julie wasn't simply lying about it for some mysterious
reason of her own,' she said, 'I can only think of one thing
it might mean.'

'That Margaret was careful to see that her papers were
in a safe place before setting fire to the house herself, but
said they were lost because that would make it seem
specially unlikely that she'd have done such a thing? Is that
what you think?'

'I think it may be what Julie wanted me to think.'

'But Margaret had an alibi for the time the fire started,
given her by Julie herself.'

'Margaret might have got someone else to do the actual
job for her.'

'Given them a key and told them to do it while she herself was safely at our party? And Emma Carey was caught up in the plot by chance, but would have been able to identify who was doing the job, and had to be locked in and horribly killed. If that's what happened, we haven't got to look for anyone with anything specially against Emma—David, for instance, or me. But we still don't know—probably we'll never know—what took her to Margaret's house.'

'I really believe my theory about that is the right one. She went there to tell Margaret you'd definitely never been married to her. She was afraid her letter to you might have done you damage with the person she called your boss, and she wanted to set things right.'

'Yes. Yes, that's probably the only answer we'll ever get.'

'It's so terrible sad. We might have got to like her if we'd been given a chance.' She gave a yawn, feeling that sleep after all might not be impossible. 'I might even get to like David if he gave us a little encouragement.'

'Don't walk into the trap,' Patrick said. 'He'd only let you down at the first possible moment. People like him aren't curable, unless perhaps they get religion. But then they're as unbearable about that as they are when they're in a state of sin. No, it's one thing for me to have a sort of affection for him, but don't let him get any hold on you. Now go to sleep.'

He gave her a kiss and let her move a little away from him. A few minutes later she was asleep and did not wake up till the alarm clock went off.

On a Monday morning they always got up earlier than on other mornings, because Patrick had a nine o'clock lecture to give. Henrietta thought that he did not look as if he had had even as much sleep as she had, and asked him if he had really got to go to the department, as work there surely would not be proceeding as usual. But he said he did not think that the burning of the Professor's house, with a murder thrown in, should be allowed to affect the fertilization of the ovum, the matter most on his mind that morning. He left as usual by car, and presently Henrietta set out with her shopping-trolley along Tenterfield Road to the supermarket near the bottom of it.

She found something oddly soothing about wandering along the alleys packed with foodstuffs, the fruit and vegetables, the shelves stacked high with tins, the packets of meat, the bread and cakes and biscuits, and she piled more than she usually did into the store's trolley that she was pushing ahead of her, and it was only when she had paid for it all, passing out at the check-out counter, and was packing what she had bought into her own trolley that a voice that she recognized accosted her.

'Why, Henrietta, I thought it was you when I saw you ahead of me, but I'm so short-sighted nowadays. I wasn't sure. What d'you say to a coffee over the way? Have you time for it?'

It was the cheerful voice of Marie Mackintosh. Henrietta had never heard it anything but cheerful. If Marie was ever visited by depression, Henrietta had never seen or heard any sign of it. Marie was about twenty years older than Henrietta, but whereas Henrietta's hair was grey already, Marie's was still naturally blonde. It was mostly hidden at the moment under a scarf tied under her plump chin. She was slightly the taller of the two women, and distinctly the broader in a well-cushioned, comfortable way which was exaggerated by the fact that she was addicted to wearing trousers. Besides these, this morning she was wearing a quilted jacket and was pushing before her a well-filled trolley.

'Yes, coffee would be nice,' Henrietta said. 'I'm not in any hurry.'

The coffee shop was across the street, and as they made their way to it, Marie chatted amiably about the difficulty that she had found in locating the shelf on which a kind of pâté that she had particularly wanted was kept.

'They keep changing things about, so that you have to
go wandering all over the place to find what you want,' she
said. 'They do it on purpose. They think it'll make you
notice new things and buy things you weren't thinking of.
And I admit it sometimes works. I've bought some frozen
coleslaw that I've never tried before. But it does waste one's
time.'

They were standing close to some traffic lights which at
that moment changed, showing the little green man who
indicated that it was time for pedestrians to cross the street.
Marie charged across it as if she feared that he might disappear before she was safely across, while Henrietta followed less dashingly behind her. They went into the
coffee-shop, sat down at one of the small tables and ordered
coffee and at Marie's insistence, some biscuits. The coffee
was pale and the milk that was served with it came in
little cartons, but at least it was hot and Henrietta found
something refreshing in the obvious fact that Marie had
not spent a night almost sleepless, filled with visions of fire
and murder. It turned out that what she wanted to talk
about was what she and her husband were going to do
when he retired.

She untied her headscarf, gave her hair a pat, stirred the
longlife milk into her coffee, and said, 'It's almost frightening, you know, to feel you've got all the time in the world
to go absolutely anywhere you want to, but that the one
thing you've still got to make up your mind about is what
you really want to do. We've been saying for a long time
that what we wanted to do was to go round the world. It
seems the obvious thing to do, doesn't it? I mean, if we put
it off, we'll get too old to tackle it. But what is there really
about going round the world, except that it sounds the sort
of thing one should have done at least once in one's life?
And even if we stick to doing that, there are two ways to
go, aren't there, eastwards or westwards? And the whole
world seems to be in such a mess these days that one wants

to be careful one doesn't land in one of the places where they're having a civil war or anything. What do you think you and Patrick will do when he retires?'

Henrietta laughed. 'That's one of the perplexing questions I've never yet asked myself, but some day I suppose we'll have to make up our minds about it.'

'Yes, it was a silly question to ask you,' Marie said. 'Of course you haven't begun to think of it yet. And you've travelled quite a lot already, haven't you?'

'Only the odd holiday in Italy and Greece and so on,' Henrietta answered. 'Nothing very enterprising. Patrick was talking yesterday about whether he should look for a new job somewhere, but I don't know how serious he really was.'

'That's very interesting.' Marie added some more sugar to what she had already put into her coffee. 'Malcolm's often said he thought Patrick was wasted here. He wouldn't be if Margaret weren't such a difficult person. Malcolm's always been able to manage her by taking no notice of her, but then she isn't afraid of him, as she is of Patrick. Malcolm's never been ambitious, and he's old and he'll soon be out of her way. But Patrick might so easily outshine her. In fact, I think he's done that already. He's sure to be made an FRS sometime soon. Of course, I don't really know about these things. I'm only quoting Malcolm. But he says if he were younger, he wouldn't stay. It was so different in the old days, when dear old Professor Ingham was head of the department. Not a brilliant man, you know —I mean scientifically, not like Margaret—but so good with people. And then, when he got old he was really quite happy to let the department run itself. Often he wouldn't put in an appearance there for days on end, and you could be sure then that if you really wanted him you'd be able to find him pottering about his garden. You should have seen his roses! As good a show as in the Botanic Garden. I often think that one of Margaret's troubles is that she really hasn't any interests outside her work, and that's why she can't help interfering with other people and trying to control everything they do. But I must say I was surprised that she'd actually got across someone so badly that they burnt her house down. I can't get over it.'

Henrietta thought that Marie looked as if she had got over it quite easily. She gave a little disapproving shake of the head, but her usual smile did not leave her face.

'But to go back to what I was saying a moment ago,' she resumed. 'If you were going round the world, would you go eastwards or westwards?'

It was a problem on which Henrietta had no opinion at all, but as Marie continued to talk about it, it became clear that she had made up her mind that the right way to go would be by Mexico and Fiji, but that Malcolm had got his heart set on making straight for Singapore. Henrietta thought that when the time came Marie would probably have her way, though it was possible that she might enjoy making a great effort of self-sacrifice and agree to Malcolm's wishes. They chatted for a little while, then had a little argument as to which of them should pay for the coffee, ending up by doing some careful arithmetic over the joint bill that was given to them so that each should pay for her own. Then they said how pleasant it had been to meet and parted at the door, going homewards in different directions.

Henrietta walked briskly, almost as if something were driving her to hurry. In fact, she had the whole day ahead of her, with nothing that needed urgently to be done when she reached home. It was almost as if by walking fast enough and reaching home very quickly she would be able to think clearly. She wanted to escape from the noise of the street into the quiet of the flat and give herself a drink. However, when she reached the gate of Curlingham House and was just about to turn into it, she found that she was not to have the quiet towards which she had been hurrying.

A car had stopped there just before she reached the gate and Neil Robarts looked out.

'Hallo, Henrietta,' he called out to her. 'Patrick in?'

'I shouldn't think so,' she answered as she came up to the car. 'He's got a lecture this morning.'

'Oh, that's finished some time ago,' he said, as he got out of the car. 'And I've been looking for him in his lab and in the Library and the Staff Club and can't find him anywhere, so I thought just possibly he might have come home.'

'It isn't likely on a Monday morning,' Henrietta replied, 'but I suppose it's possible. Come up and see.'

'May I?' He locked the door of the car and took hold of her trolley, preparing to drag it up the stairs for her. 'Something's come up that I wanted to discuss with him. Something I've been expecting, but I find it difficult to think about it with things at the department in the state they are. We're all doing our best to keep things there normal, but of course the students are all wildly excited and the VC's been in to try to find out what's really been going on. He came to offer Margaret his sympathy, but she wasn't anywhere around, but also he wanted to say that he doesn't like being bothered by the police. Not that he said that in so many words. He was all for being co-operative. But he seemed to imply that we ought to keep our fires and murders to ourselves.'

The Vice Chancellor of whom he had been speaking was Sir Leonard Milton, once a distinguished mathematician, but for some years now lost to mathematics in the toils of administration. He was a small—and to all appearances an unassuming—man, but one who had a will of iron and a total inability to endure being contradicted. Robarts seemed to be talking more than he normally did about anything and there was a look almost of animation on his heavy, pallid face which indicated an unusual degree of excitement in him. In fact, he went on talking all the way

up the stairs to the Careys' flat about how difficult it had
been to persuade the students that the corpse in Professor
Franks's house had not been hers, for she had not been into
the department that morning, in itself a most troublesome
thing at the moment, though he realized that she had had
to go shopping to buy herself some clothes. That, at least,
was what Julie Bishop had said she had been doing, and
he presumed that it took precedence over dealing with the
VC, which had fallen mostly on Robarts himself, a task he
had not enjoyed. They reached the first floor landing and
Henrietta unlocked the door of the flat.

Going in, she called out, 'Patrick!'

There was no reply and as she invited Robarts in she
said, 'It doesn't look as if he's here.'

And indeed he was not. A note in Patrick's handwriting
had been left propped up against the clock on the sitting-
room mantelpiece. It said. *Gone to London. Back this evening,
or will phone. P.*

She looked at it in bewilderment, showing it to Robarts.

'London,' she said. 'What on earth is he doing in
London?'

'He didn't tell you he meant to go?' Robarts said.

'Not a word.'

'Does he often do that sort of thing?'

'No, not really. He can be a bit unpredictable sometimes,
but I think it means something very important has come
up.' She did not say that she believed it must have something to do with his brother.

'I tell you what, then,' Robarts said with a sudden wide
smile that somehow did not fit his face, 'you're all alone,
aren't you? You must come to lunch with us. Lydia will be
so pleased to see you.'

The Robartses went in so little for hospitality that for a
moment Henrietta felt that he could not mean what he had
said. But he continued to smile at her and showed no sign

of withdrawing his invitation. Curious how Lydia would really react to the appearance of an unexpected visitor, she decided to accept it and, keeping him waiting only while she unpacked her trolley in the kitchen, she rejoined him and the two of them went down to his car.

The Robartses lived in a bungalow a mile or so further from the centre of the town than the Careys. The bungalow was in a housing development that had been built only about five years before. It had a base of red brick with weather tiles above it, and a steep pitched roof pierced by the one window of an attic. The garden was enclosed by a privet hedge and, desolate though it was in February, was extremely neat with a paved path up to the front door bordered by straight rows of wallflowers promising to burst into bloom when the weather warmed up. The building had a car-port and Robarts drove into it, scrambled out of the car and hurried round it to open the door for Henrietta. Their arrival was greeted by noisy, excited barking inside the house, and when he opened the front door the small Cairn-like dog with which Henrietta and Patrick had seen the Robartses in the Botanic Garden came racing out to meet them, pausing when he saw Henrietta and giving Henrietta's ankles careful investigation before he appeared sure that it was advisable to allow her to enter the house.

Only a moment after the dog, Lydia appeared, wearing a plastic apron over her dark trousers and scarlet sweater and holding a saucepan in one hand and a wooden spoon in the other.

'Oh,' she said on seeing Henrietta. 'Oh.' It seemed to embarrass her that both her hands were full and that she could not hold out one to shake Henrietta's. 'I wondered . . .' she remarked, an incomplete sort of statement.

As always, when she stood near her husband, she achieved the air of making him look very short and stocky, while she herself seemed as if unnaturally lengthened out.

'I brought Henrietta home for lunch,' he said, but seemed to think no other explanation necessary.

'Oh. I wondered why Tarquin was barking so noisily,' Lydia Robarts went on. She seemed to find it easier to accept Henrietta's arrival if she did not actually look at her. 'He doesn't usually make such a noise when you arrive on your own, dear. Wonderful he is at knowing if there's a stranger about. We need never be afraid of burglars while we've got him.'

'If my coming like this is awfully inconvenient, do just tell me,' Henrietta said. 'Neil could just drop me at home again.'

'No, no, oh no!' Lydia said. 'It's only shepherd's pie, but I don't suppose you'll mind that. I'm just making the sauce for the cauliflower. You'll excuse me, won't you?' Making an explanatory gesture with her saucepan and spoon she disappeared into the kitchen.

Robarts took Henrietta into the living-room, followed closely and still suspiciously by Tarquin, the dog. He soon made himself comfortable on the hearth, however.

The room was long and narrow, with a large, double-glazed window at each end of it and with more ornaments in the way of china and glass vases and bowls and dishes than Henrietta could remember ever having seen in a room before. They were ranged along the shelves of a dresser and along shelves where books might have been expected to be, and in a glass-fronted corner cabinet, and everything glittered with cleanliness. One of the Robartses or perhaps the two together, must spend a fair amount of their free time in the house simply dusting, polishing, washing. The easy chairs were covered in very fresh-looking cretonne and the brightly patterned carpet looked as if the vacuum cleaner had only just gone over it.

Robarts waved Henrietta to a chair and, opening a cupboard, brought out sherry and glasses.

'I believe this is the first time you've been here,' he said.

'We don't socialize very much. And when I think how often we've been to your house, I feel ashamed. But Lydia's very shy, you know. Afraid her standards aren't up to other people's. I hope you can drink medium.'

Since there was no question of choice, Henrietta accepted her glass of medium sherry, trying to make up her mind as she did so why Robarts had really brought her here.

'I'm sorry you've missed Patrick,' she said. 'Was it something very urgent you wanted to see him about?'

'Well, fairly so,' he answered. 'I wanted to ask his advice. He understands Margaret so much better than I do and there's something I've got to put to her, and fairly soon too, and I thought he might be able to tell me whether or not he thinks I should go about it now, the situation being what it is and her mind certainly occupied with all her own problems, or whether I should risk waiting. It would be a bit of a risk, and it would be very unfortunate for us if things went wrong.'

'Is it about that Chair you were telling us about yesterday?' Henrietta asked. 'Do you think she's going to get the extra one for the department and offer it to you?'

'It's only partly about that,' he said. 'No, it's really about a job at Berkeley—*Darling!*' He suddenly raised his voice and shouted. 'Don't you want some sherry?'

'In a moment, in a moment,' Lydia's reply came faintly from the kitchen. 'Don't wait for me. I don't want this sauce to spoil.'

'The fact is, I had a telephone call this morning from Berkeley,' he went on, 'and I've got to give them an answer pretty quickly.'

'You had a call from someone in Berkeley itself?' Henrietta felt impressed although she knew that transatlantic calls could go through as easily as calls to London. 'Their clocks are way behind ours. Someone must have got up awfully early there if you got a call from them in the morning.'

At that moment Lydia came into the room. She chose a
chair slightly behind her husband's, and from that place of
safety she began to talk. Once started, there seemed to be
no stopping her. As she talked on and on, Henrietta took
in the fact that Lydia was one of those people who must
have the floor entirely to themselves, one who finds it not
worth their while simply to take part in a conversation.
Henrietta had always supposed that silence was natural to
Lydia, but now she began to understand that it came
merely as a stop-gap between attacks of speech.

'Neil has been telling you about our going to America,
hasn't he?' she said. 'I heard him. Of course, it's very
important to us, and this time we aren't going to let Margaret wreck it for us. Did you know she did that before? It
was only a short time after she'd got here. We had the thing
about fixed up—it was in Texas that time—and Professor
Ingham had only just retired. Of course, if he hadn't,
there'd have been no problem. He had a very high opinion
of Neil and always did everything in his power to promote
him. And we did so want to go. It wasn't just the higher
salary and having the status of a professor and so on, it
was getting away from this awful place where people, it
sometimes seems to me, are hardly human. They're so
unfriendly. We've been here ten years and during all that
time I honestly believe we haven't made a single friend.
We'll meet new people, when they come, and be as hospit-
able to them as is reasonable, and we think oh, here's someone nice, we're going to get along splendidly, and then,
believe it or not, we never see them again. I don't understand it. It's something in the atmosphere. So we've always
wanted to go to America, because we've been told people
are so much friendlier there than they are here. But that
isn't the main point, though of course it's very important.
The thing we've been wondering about is how to handle
Margaret, because of how she wrecked our chance of going
last time. It was all almost fixed up and we'd even been

making inquiries about how to get our furniture moved, when suddenly the whole thing was called off. And it was only because Neil met one of the people from Texas at a conference later that we ever found out why—'

'Darling,' Robarts interrupted, 'it really isn't necessary to go into all that.'

As if he had not spoken, she swept on. 'You see, someone over there had made some inquiries about Neil from Margaret, and she'd said—yes, that frightful woman had actually said—a most awful thing about Neil. She'd accused him of plagiarizing some technique that covered his own approach to a problem. Of stealing someone else's work, that's to say! Can you imagine it? But perhaps I shouldn't be calling her a frightful woman to you. Perhaps you're one of her admirers. Of course, everyone knows she's crazy about Patrick and that he doesn't exactly reciprocate, which makes her furious. But he might be able to advise Neil how he should approach her, so that she doesn't play the same trick again. That talk of hers, of getting a Chair for him here, of course that's all nonsense. Why should she do that if she believes he steals other people's work, unless it's just to score off Patrick? Now do tell me something I'm longing to know. Do you believe she thinks it was Patrick who tried to kill her on Saturday night? Or does she think it was Neil, because of course Neil's the more obvious with his definite offer that's come through from Berkeley this morning. That man Heinzman said it was coming, and if there was a chance that Margaret might spoil it again she'd be worth murdering, that's my opinion. Of course it's obvious that—'

'Darling!' Robarts broke in again more firmly. 'Nobody tried to kill Margaret on Saturday. They killed a poor unfortunate woman from Aberdeen.'

She waved a hand as if she was brushing aside the interruption.

'Isn't it obvious whoever did it thought he was locking

Margaret into that room, and was going to kill her in the fire,' she ran on. 'With the curtains drawn and a light on inside, how could he tell one woman from another, and wasn't Margaret the one he'd have expected to see there? And you may never have noticed it, but the curtains at the windows of that room weren't particularly thick, so he'd have been able to see that there was someone there, a woman, but not really who it was. Oh, I'm sure Margaret knows someone tried to murder her and she has probably made up her mind by now who it was, even if she hasn't any proof, but she'll have her revenge somehow.'

'Perhaps it's an extraordinary thing,' Henrietta said, managing to insert a few words into Lydia's flow of speech, 'but it's never occurred to me that the intended victim of the fire was Margaret.'

'Of course it was, of course it was. Oh God, I've been forgetting!' Lydia had suddenly remembered the shepherd's pie in her oven, perhaps growing too brown by now, abandoned what she had been about to say next and jumped up and hurried from the room.

But once the three of them were seated at the dining-table and the shepherd's pie had been placed before them with the cauliflower, the sauce over which had dried to a slimy skin, Lydia picked up her sentence where she had broken it off and talked on until they had eaten the stewed apples and custard that had followed the pie, drunk some instant coffee, and Henrietta had said firmly that she really must get home.

Neil, with a sullen look on his face that suited it better than the smiling geniality that he had tried to assume when he was inviting her to lunch, drove her home. They were silent almost all the way and Henrietta had seldom felt how blessed a thing it could be to be free from the sound of a human voice. She thought that the fact that Lydia had been unable to find friends in Knotlington was not surprising and she felt more sympathy for Neil's sombrely stolid manner than she ever had before.

In the sitting-room she lit the gas fire and sat down beside it. The quiet of the flat was very soothing. But there on the mantelpiece, where Patrick had propped it against the clock, was still his message. *Gone to London. Back this evening, or will phone. P.* She wondered if he had tried to phone during the time that she had been out, but if he had, no doubt he would try again. More probably he would come home on one of the late trains. There was one that reached Knotlington only a little before midnight. She had not had much time to think about why he should suddenly have gone to London. If she had come home after doing her shopping, instead of having coffee with Marie Mackintosh, he would certainly have told her. But whatever had taken him, he must have been in a hurry to catch the midday train, or he would have written a little more about his reason for going.

She supposed it was something to do with David. Perhaps David had phoned, wanting Patrick to come to him, to help him perhaps with money, perhaps just with advice. Perhaps even offering to go to the police with his story, if Patrick would go with him to give him some support. But if that had been the case, it would have made better sense for David to return to Knotlington than for Patrick to go to London. She decided that that was unlikely. It might be that David had done no more than drop an unwary remark that had made Patrick believe that he would be able to find him.

Meanwhile there was the theory to think about, suggested by Lydia, that the intended victim of the murder in Margaret Franks's house had been Margaret herself and not Emma Carey. If it should be correct, one thing that it meant was that David had had nothing to do with it. For Margaret meant nothing to him whatever. He could have had no conceivable reason for wanting to burn her house down or for making sure that a woman whom he supposed to be Margaret should die in the fire. If David had been involved, then he had known that his victim would be the woman he had married. But what an incredibly complicated way of committing a murder it would have been, how easily it might have failed, and for what possible reason could he have wanted to murder the poor woman? She could do him no harm, even if, as she had, she had discovered the truth about his deception of her concerning his identity?

Then suddenly Henrietta thought of a motive he might have had for wanting her dead.

Suppose he had married again. Some people appeared to have been ready to believe that Patrick had committed bigamy and it had been easy enough to prove that he was innocent. The woman herself had protested almost indignantly that he was not the man whom she had married. But was there anything unlikely about David's having done that very thing? Marrying women, perhaps several at a time, living on them, then when there was a risk that they might bring this to light, somehow disposing of them, seemed something that David just possibly might do. And if some knowledge of this, perhaps only some hint, had reached Patrick that morning, it could certainly explain why he had taken off so immediately for London.

But what about the theory that the woman who had been meant to die in the blaze had been Margaret Franks?

There was a good deal of plausibility about it. As a figure seen only through curtains, she and Emma Carey would not have been utterly unlike. They both were tall, well-built women and both had bobbed hair. Their outlines would not have been impossibly dissimilar. But now the question of motive became too complicated. Someone, Henrietta thought, might have decided to set Margaret's house on fire as an act of revenge for one of the unkind things that she was only too often capable of doing. An act of spite, or revenge, with no intention at the outset of committing murder. Was she not almost certainly going to be away from her home, as she had accepted an invitation to drinks at the Careys' flat? But after all, it appeared that she had not gone to the party, she was there at her enemy's mercy, and suddenly the temptation had become too much for him and he had turned the key on her, locked her in with the flames that he brought into being, before escaping himself by the door in the basement that opened out into the yard that led to the lane behind the house.

Yes, but how had he got in?

He had used a Yale key which he must somehow have obtained from Margaret herself, or perhaps from Mrs Digby, and he had dropped that key into a little Chelsea bowl in the Careys' flat. And he had come to their party and there had come face to face with the woman whom he believed he had killed. Who had he been? Neil Robarts? Simon Quinn? Malcolm Mackintosh? Charles Hedden? Even Dr Heinzman from Berkeley, though that seemed farfetched. And could the key possibly have been deposited where it was by Julie Bishop, who had an alibi for the time of the murder, or so Margaret Franks herself had said, establishing her own alibi, but who might just possibly have been in league with one of the others?

How long Henrietta sat by the hissing gas fire, going over and over all the thoughts that came into her head, she did not know. She did not notice that the early winter twilight had come, and then the darkness outside the window. In the room itself, only the gas jets made a little light and it was not until it occurred to her to wonder what the time was and whether it might not be a good idea to make a cup of tea that she thought of moving. But it was not that that brought her suddenly to her feet, startled and for no special reason apprehensive. It was the ringing of the front doorbell.

It was a very urgent ringing. Someone kept his finger on

the bell for much longer than necessary, and then rang it a second time and pounded on the door with the knocker there.

Henrietta switched on the light in the sitting-room, fled to the hall to stop the terrible clatter, switched on the light there and flung the door open.

Charles Hedden, of whom she had been thinking only a little while before, stood there. His face was white and his thick grey hair was on end. She thought he was trembling.

'Where's Patrick, Henrietta?' he asked in a hoarse voice. 'Isn't he here?'

'No, he's in London,' she answered.

'Oh God, this is awful, I don't want to tell you, but I'll have to. The Franks woman is down there in the street. In the gutter. Dead. I think she's been run over.'

# *Eight*

It was raining. Henrietta did not know when it had started. She had not noticed it. But it must have been some time ago, for puddles had already formed on the uneven paving of the path that led to the gate. There was a chill in the air that was far sharper than when she had come home in the afternoon.

Just outside the gate there was a street-lamp, and its light fell on something that sprawled in the gutter, a dreadful shape, frightening in its stillness. Henrietta could feel her heart pounding and she had difficulty in breathing as she followed Charlie Hedden out into the street. Margaret Franks lay there on her side, her arms flung out above her head as if she was trying to grasp at something that was not there. Her legs were separated, one half bent under her, the other sticking out sideways in an impossible posture. She was wearing the grey suit that she had worn when she had come to the Careys' flat on Saturday evening, but it was sodden with the rain. Her hair clung wetly to her head. There was blood on the back of her head and smeared down her neck and collar. Her handbag lay in the gutter.

A few feet away from her was Charlie Hedden's car. Its headlights were on, helping the street-lamp to light up the scene. As he and Henrietta passed through the gate he kept a tight hold of her arm.

'I moved her,' he said in a half-whisper. 'She was lying on her face and I felt I had to make sure . . . But as soon as I touched her I knew . . . It's so horrible. I thought I was going to vomit, then I thought I'd got to get hold of Patrick or Quinn, and someone had got to get the police.'

Where Henrietta stood, the ground seemed strangely unsteady under her. It seemed to be twisting and turning

in a way that made it very difficult for her to stay on her
feet and she still found it hard to get her breath. She held
on to the gate to steady herself.

'If she was run over . . .' she began, than paused.

'Yes?' Charlie said.

'Where was the car going? This is a dead end. It doesn't
lead anywhere.'

'I suppose it came up here by mistake, then turned and
drove off as fast as it could.'

'We've got to get the police.'

'All right. You go. I'll stay here with her.'

It was not only the cold rain that stung on her face and
was beginning to penetrate the sweater that she was wearing that made Henrietta glad to turn and run into the
house. The door of Charlie's flat was open, a light was on
inside and she could see a telephone on a bureau in his
living-room. Because it would save her staggering unstead-
ily up the stairs to the flat above, she went in and dialled
999. But it seemed a long time, and there seemed to be a
maddening number of people with whom she had to speak
before she at last managed to be put in touch with Detective-Inspector Brightmore. When at last she achieved this,
however, his reactions were satisfactorily rapid. He asked
hardly any questions, but told her to make sure a watch
was kept on the street, rain or not, and that he would arrive
in a very few minutes.

She put down the telephone and stayed rigidly still for a
moment, but she was beginning to get over the first effects
of shock, and when she noticed an umbrella in Charlie's
hall, it occurred to her to take it out to him.

'Thanks,' he said as she opened it for him and he took
cover under it, 'but you go inside. No point in both of us
getting wet. Now what about a doctor?'

'He wouldn't be able to do anything for her,' she said.
'Let's leave that to the police.'

He stood looking down at the body in the road.

'Margaret,' he said softly. 'Oh, Margaret.'

Something about the way he said it took Henrietta by surprise and made her linger, wondering if he was going to say any more. It told her a great deal about something of which she had never even dreamt and filled her with a new kind of shock.

But when he went on, all he said was, 'Go on, go inside. Stay in my flat. It'll be more accessible than yours when the police get here.'

She saw the sense of that and went back to his flat. But once she was in it, leaving the door standing open, she began to think it would have been better to go upstairs, because she knew where the whisky was kept and this seemed to her a moment when it would be very welcome. However, there was no problem about finding whisky in Charlie's flat. There was a bottle with a tumbler beside it on a table with a word-processor on it and a portable telephone and a scattered mess of papers. Not wasting time looking for a clean tumbler, she sloshed some whisky into the one that was on the table, and drank it neat. She began by sipping it, then found herself gulping it, as it sent a fiery warmth through her, making her forget that her hair and her face were wet and that her sweater was clinging damply to her. She stood looking around her with the kind of wonder that she always felt when she entered this room. It was by far the best room in the whole house, with a high ceiling with a handsomely moulded cornice, tall windows, some fine built-in bookcases, and a fireplace which, being Victorian, was rather overpowering, the carved overmantel reaching almost to the ceiling, yet which had distinct dignity. But it was always in a condition of near squalor and but for the fact that it was firmly cleaned by Mrs Forbes, who had been to Henrietta that morning and would be coming to Charlie next day, would soon have degenerated into a slum. It was easy to imagine insects settling happily among the scattered papers and books and odd articles of clothing that lay around, leading their undisturbed lives there. Henrietta shuddered faintly as she thought of it. Yet it was the room of a man who appeared to be very contented with what he had and wanted no changes made.

It was not long before she heard the sounds of cars arriving, then men's voices and then Charlie coming by himself into the flat. He left the umbrella open on the floor in the hall to dry and made straight for the bottle of whisky. But seeing that Henrietta had appropriated his glass, he went to a cupboard, took out another and gave himself a generous quantity of whisky and gulped it, all without speaking. Then he drew a deep breath and said, 'Why don't you sit down?'

It had not occurred to Henrietta till then that there was no reason why she should remain standing in the middle of that shambles of a room, but she had simply not thought of sitting down. However, she moved towards a chair now, which was covered in some ancient, faded, flowered material and which obviously had a broken spring in the seat. Charlie dropped down on to a divan covered in an old striped blanket.

'So you and Margaret were lovers once,' she said as she sat down.

Charlie showed no sign of surprise at the remark.

'For a little while,' he said. 'A long time ago. Soon after she came here.'

'Why did it stop?'

'Oh, it didn't really suit either of us,' he answered. 'We liked each other, but sex, you know, that was different. At the time it seemed logical that we should have an affair, but it wasn't really what we wanted. But we stayed quite good friends though we saw less and less of each other as time went on. You know how that happens.'

'I don't really,' Henrietta said. 'But I've never had an affair for logical reasons. Are there a lot of men out there?'

'Yes, with that man Brightmore in charge and he said

he'd be coming in shortly to ask us a few things. At the moment they're erecting barriers all round the spot.'

'Have they—have they moved her?'

'Not yet and they told me I shouldn't have moved her either, once I was sure she was dead, because if I hadn't they might have been able to tell whether she was killed before or after the rain began. If I hadn't touched her, you see, the ground underneath her might have stayed dry and that would have meant that it happened before the rain had started, but if it was wet it would have meant it had happened later. But with me having moved her, the spot where she was lying got soaked from the water in the gutter.'

'But won't a pathologist be able to tell them when she died?'

'More or less, but I don't think they can ever be absolutely accurate.'

'When did the rain start?' Henrietta asked. 'I didn't notice it myself.'

'About half past five, I think. It was about six when I started home from the Library, where I'd been spending the afternoon, and it had been raining for some time by then. The roads were quite wet. But I can't say for certain either.'

'I wonder if Simon's home yet. Do you think we ought to go up and see? If he's there he ought to be told what's happened.'

Charlie nodded thoughtfully, but then shook his head, reaching for the whisky and beginning to pour out some more for himself, then, remembering that he had a guest, held the bottle out to her. She let him give her some more, and sipped it gratefully.

'Well, do we fetch Simon?' she asked.

'I'd be inclined to leave it to the police,' he said. 'My impression is that the less we interfere in anything, the better. Perhaps I ought not to have brought you down, but the fact is I was so dead scared I couldn't stay out there by myself. And it was Patrick I was after. I wonder if Margaret knew he wasn't here.'

'If she did, I don't know what brought her,' Henrietta said. 'She wasn't very likely to be coming to see me or Simon.'

'So probably she didn't know—' He broke off as a voice from the open door into the hall called out, 'Dr Hedden!'

He sprang up and went to the door. It was Detective-Inspector Brightmore there, accompanied by Detective-Sergeant Dance. Charlie brought them into the living-room, but either because the level of the whisky bottle was low, or because he believed that the police did not drink while on duty, did not offer any to them. Both men were in anoraks, darkened by their wetness, with the hoods up over their heads. They shook them back and Brightmore said, 'Mind if we take them off?' And without waiting for an answer he unzipped his coat and pulled it off. Dance did the same.

'There are a few things we'd better ask you straight away,' Brightmore said, 'although we'll go into things more thoroughly later. Hasn't your husband come home yet, Mrs Carey?'

'He's in London,' Henrietta answered. 'He'll probably get back later in the evening.'

'Sit down,' Charlie said to the two men and himself resumed his seat on the divan. 'We'll both help you in any way we can. We don't know if Quinn's in. We haven't been up to see.'

They found chairs that were not buried in books and papers, but, looking around them, gave themselves a moment to take in the way that Charles Hedden lived before beginning their questions. There would be a fair number of these, Henrietta realized, and she was prepared for the first one that came. It was one that she expected.

'Hadn't the Professor a car, Dr Hedden?' Brightmore

asked. 'She wouldn't have walked up here all the way from the University, would she?'

'No, she'd no car,' Charlie answered. 'I don't know how she got here. She just might have walked. She used to walk from her own home to the University, but of course that wasn't as long a distance as this would have been. But it's more likely someone gave her a lift, or else that she took a taxi. A lift, I think, is the more probable.'

'From someone who just put her down at the gate and then killed her?'

'That's more likely, isn't it, than that a taxi-driver did it. Or have you any mad taxi-drivers in Knotlington? Have you had any other suspicious cases of violence where a taxi-driver might have been involved?'

'Now, now, Dr Hedden, don't take me up like that. I agree with you that a lift from someone she thought was a friend is the most probable explanation of how she got here. But do you know why she came? What brought her?'

Charlie looked at Henrietta, waiting for her to answer the question.

She said, 'I can only think she was coming to see us— that's to say, probably my husband. What happened on Saturday must have left her with a terrible lot of things to sort out in her own affairs, and she may have wanted him to take some things in her department off her hands for a time. But I'm only guessing.'

'You say he's in London,' Brightmore said. 'Do you know what took him there?'

'As a matter of fact, I don't,' she answered. 'I went out shopping this morning and then had coffee with a friend, and when I got home I found a note on our mantelpiece which simply said, "Gone to London. Back this evening, or will phone." He hasn't phoned yet, so I imagine he'll get home presently.'

'Would it have had anything to do with his brother?' Brightmore asked.

'It might have, but I simply don't know.'

'Is it the sort of thing he often did?'

'I can't remember his ever having done it before.'

'So you've no certainty at the moment that he actually went.'

She stared at him wide-eyed for a moment, before the meaning of what he had said actually sank in.

'Inspector, if what you're suggesting is that it was my husband who drove Professor Franks here, killed her and then vanished away, having set up some sort of alibi in London, perhaps with that brother of his, you're really wasting your time,' she said indignantly. 'If you've any doubts, go and look in our garage. I think you'll find our car there. He must have gone to the station by taxi. And what a crazy thing it would have been to do, to bring her to our very gate and kill her here, of all places.'

'You're going too fast for me, Mrs Carey,' Brightmore said, with a faint twitch of his lips which might have been intended as an apologetic smile. 'As it happens, we've looked in the garage already, and there are two cars there, yours and one that I presume belongs to Mr Quinn. And both are dry, and there are no muddy tyre-marks on the floor of the garage, so at least both cars were driven in, whenever it was, before the rain began. But I'm not sug-gesting that your husband didn't go to London. I'm only trying to find out what we know precisely and what may be only supposition. It won't be until later this evening that we'll know for certain if your husband went to London. Now, talking of Mr Quinn, do you happen to know if he's at home or not?'

Henrietta shook her head and Charlie said, 'We were talking about that just before you came in, Inspector. We were discussing whether or not we should go up to tell him what's happened, then we thought we'd better leave that to you in case you thought we were taking too much on ourselves. Actually, if he's home, you'd think the noise out there would have brought him down to find out what was happening, so perhaps he isn't at home. But you say his car's in the garage.'

'And has been there, as I said, since before the rain began, which was about five-thirty. Bob—' He turned to Detective-Sergeant Dance. 'Go up, will you, and see if Mr Quinn is in, and if he is, bring him down.'

The Sergeant got to his feet and went out.

As he went, Charlie said, 'There's something I've been wanting to ask you, Inspector. Was it actually being struck by a car that killed Professor Franks?'

Brightmore did not answer immediately. He leant forward, rubbing his knees with his hands and looking down at them. The small, deep-set eyes in his thin, haggard face seemed to see nothing.

At last he said, 'It's early days to say. It doesn't look very likely.'

'Why not?' Charlie asked.

'Because it looks as if what killed her was a violent blow on the back of the head,' Brightmore said. 'A queer thing to happen, unless perhaps she was already lying in the road when the car hit her. But I'm not offering any opinion at the moment. That's the job of the forensic people.'

'You think someone drove her up here, let her get out of the car, then struck her on the back of the head with a so-called blunt instrument?'

'Could be.'

It was obvious that Charlie was not going to get any more than that out of the Inspector.

'It seems to me,' Henrietta said, 'that the person we want here is Julie.'

The Inspector looked up quickly. 'Julie? Would that be Miss Bishop, Professor Frank's secretary?'

'Yes,' Henrietta answered. 'She saw more of her than anyone else in the department. She may even have seen

who it was she drove away with, if it's true that she came
up here in the car of some friend.'

'Where does this Miss Bishop live?' Brightmore asked.

'With her parents, in Cardingley.' Cardingley was one
of the suburbs of Knotlington. 'Shall I telephone her and
ask her to come here, or would you sooner speak to her
yourself?'

'I'd be grateful if you'd do that,' Brightmore said. 'She's
got a car, has she?'

'Yes.' Henrietta got up to go to the telephone, but
paused. 'I tell her what's happened, do I?'

'Why not, since you've got to give a reason for wanting
her to come here so urgently.'

Henrietta nodded and went to the telephone on the
bureau from which she had earlier dialled the police.

It happened that she knew the Bishop family's number,
and her call was answered almost immediately by Julie's
father. Henrietta told him who she was and asked if she
could speak to Julie.

After a brief pause Julie's voice, sounding impatient, said,
'Yes?'

'Julie, this is Henrietta speaking. Can you come here
now—immediately? I'm sorry, but it's urgent.' Henrietta
was wishing that the Inspector had taken it on himself to
summon Julie. She could not think of what to say that
would make what had happened sound in the least real.
She could not simply say that there had been a murder and
that Julie's presence was required on the scene. 'A terrible
thing has happened,' she managed to go on. 'Professor
Franks has been found dead in the road just outside our
gate and the police are here—'

'Dead?' Julie's voice squealed at her down the telephone.
'You said dead?'

'Yes.'

'And the police are there?'

'Yes.'

'It's murder, then?'

'It looks like it.'

'Oh, I knew it would happen—I knew it!' Julie cried. 'I told her she was in danger, but she wouldn't listen to me. And you want me to come over? I'll come immediately. Tell the policemen I'm coming. It won't take me long. And if I can help to do anything to nail the bastard who did it to her, I'll do it. I'm going to be able to tell them a thing or two.'

Henrietta put down the telephone and returned to the chair where she had been sitting.

'Could you hear most of that, Inspector?' she asked. 'Or do you want me to tell you what she said?'

'I heard most of it, I think,' he replied. 'But I wouldn't mind a repetition from you to make sure I got it right.'

'She said she's going to be able to tell you a thing or two,' Henrietta said. 'Also she said she knew the murder was going to happen and that she'd warned Professor Franks that she was in danger.'

He nodded, but without looking much interested.

'I've talked to her already, of course, about her having driven Professor Franks up here the evening of the fire,' he said, 'and she didn't say anything then about expecting a murder. There's a habit a lot of people have of being wise after the event.'

'If it was a case of that, she reacted very quickly,' Henrietta said. 'But have you talked to Mrs Robarts?'

'Yes, and her husband too,' he answered. 'Why?'

'It's just that she seems to have got the idea that when the door was locked in that burning house, whoever did it believed that it was Professor Franks who was shut in the room, not Emma Carey.'

'Oh, we'd thought of that ourselves,' he said with a faint sound of ironic amusement in his voice. 'We may even have been responsible for putting it in her mind.'

'And now that Professor Franks has been killed here at our gate, you're quite sure you were right,' she said. 'You don't believe my brother-in-law David murdered his wife.'

'I can only say that if he did it, he chose about the most complicated way of doing a murder that I've ever heard of —Ah, here's Mr Quinn.'

Simon had just shot into the room in his usual precipitate fashion, then came to a dead stop in the middle of it, looking round wildly at each of the three people there in turn, as if he had to make sure which of them was a policeman. His little, sharp-featured face was very pale.

'I'm sorry Rachel couldn't come down,' he said, his voice a nervous croak. 'She can't leave Tessa. But you could go up to her if you want to. Of course we knew that something awful had happened. All those lights in the street—we could see them from our window—and all the cars and the policemen and the noise. I'd have come down to see what it was, only Rachel persuaded me to wait till you sent for me, if I was wanted. But I didn't dream of anything so awful—I mean, the thing happening to someone one knows, and someone as special as Professor Franks. But that's callous, isn't it, because it would be awful for anyone, whoever it was? We thought it was just an accident, though, a hit-and-run sort of thing, though that was puzzling, because of this road being a dead end. We couldn't think of any reason why anyone should be driving up here so fast that they'd hit a pedestrian. You'd have expected them to slow down before they reached the top, even supposing they'd turned into it by mistake and thought there was a way through. But if it's murder—' He stopped as abruptly as he had begun.

'Perhaps you can help us, Mr Quinn,' Brightmore said. 'You were in the Department of Biochemistry this afternoon, were you?'

'Yes.' Simon was still standing rigidly stiff in the middle of the room.

'Did you see Professor Franks at any time?'

Simon's wide forehead wrinkled. 'Yes. I think so. Did I, though? Let me think. Yes, of course I did. She came in for a few minutes when we were having tea. She didn't stay long. She obviously had something on her mind. Can you wonder? I mean none of us did wonder, knowing about her house and the dead woman in it and all that. None of us stayed long. I mean, the atmosphere wasn't—well, you know what I mean. I went back to the lab and finished a job I was doing and then came home.'

'Was that before the rain started?' Brightmore asked.

'The rain?' Simon said, as if this were a thing very seldom heard of in Knotlington. 'Oh, the rain. Yes, it was.'

'But did you see Professor Franks between your tea-time and the time you left for home?'

'Did I, now?' Simon said. 'No.'

'Are you sure of that?'

'Quite sure. Yes, I think so.'

Charlie patted the striped blanket beside him on the divan on which he was sitting. 'Come and sit down, Simon.'

Simon gave him a startled look, as if he had only just become aware of his presence, then moved swiftly to Charlie's side and sat down abruptly on the divan. Once seated, he nodded his head earnestly.

'She'd said something over tea about wanting to see me later, but when I went to her room, she'd gone.'

'Left the department, d'you mean?'

'Oh, I don't know. She may have been in Dr Robarts's lab, or have come up here already—no, she couldn't have done that, could she, or I'd have seen her when I got home. That's to say . . .' He paused.

'Yes?' Brightmore said.

'I was only thinking—but that's impossible.'

'Just give us the benefit of your thoughts, Mr Quinn, however impossible or improbable they may seem to you,' Brightmore said drily.

'I only wondered if she could have come up here to see Dr Carey,' Simon said. 'He hasn't been in the department since the morning. He came in to give a nine o'clock lecture, then he vanished. But if he'd come home, Mrs Carey would have told you about that already, wouldn't she, though of course Professor Franks might have thought he was at home. And even if she did that, it doesn't answer the question of how she got here, which I suppose is what you really want to know.'

'There's some reason to believe Dr Carey has spent most of the day in London,' Brightmore said. 'And as to the question of how Professor Franks got here, can you tell us anything about that?'

Simon gave a solemn shake of his head. 'No.'

'You didn't catch sight of her leaving the department with anybody?'

'No.'

'Who most often drove her if she wanted to get somewhere a little too far off for her to walk?'

'Oh, any of us. Anyone who could manage it. Sometimes students, even. A good many of them have cars. Or she'd phone for a taxi. But if it was just a case of going home, she'd walk.'

'This is a little too far for her to have walked, isn't it?'

'Just a bit. But it's not impossible. She was a very vigorous sort of person, you know. She might have made up her mind she'd like to do some walking while she did some thinking.'

'And then just unfortunately fell in with someone who wanted her dead and happened to have a blunt instrument handy.'

'Oh, I know I'm talking nonsense, Inspector.' Simon's voice shook almost as if he might be about to sob. 'But I can't tell you who drove her up here. The likeliest people are either Miss Bishop or Dr Robarts. I know they were

still in the department when I left. But I didn't see either
of them even talking to her.'

'How do you know they were still in the department
when you left?'

'I saw their cars in the car park.'

'I see. Well, thank you for being so helpful, Mr Quinn.
Just one thing more. How well did you know the Professor?'

Simon frowned. 'Personally, do you mean, or are you
talking about her professional side?'

'Personally, I meant.'

Simon gave a small, wry smile. 'As someone very junior
knows the boss,' he answered.

'It's sometimes someone very junior who knows what
other people are saying about the boss,' Brightmore said.
'If I were to ask you if you have any opinion as to who
might have had a motive to murder Professor Franks, would
you say you've heard anything in the way of departmental
gossip that might be helpful?'

For an instant, very fleetingly, Simon glanced at Henrietta, then with a sudden flush appearing on his cheeks, he
stared down at the floor.

'No,' he muttered.

Henrietta was sure that the Inspector had seen the glance
and a wave of anger washed through her. She did not
believe that Simon thought that she herself could have committed the murder of Margaret Franks, but she thought
the glance implied suspicion of Patrick, whether it was a
suspicion which he had formed himself in the last few
minutes, or the kind of thing that was discussed by Patrick's
colleagues. But she did not protest. It was easiest and probably wisest to say nothing, and in any case, she would
not have had much opportunity to speak just then, for a
uniformed constable came into the room and told the
Inspector that a Miss Bishop had arrived by car and asked
if he should let her in.

'Yes, certainly,' Brightmore said, and a moment later

Julie Bishop darted into the room, went to Henrietta, put her arms around her and kissed her suddenly on the cheek.

'Oh, Henrietta, I'm so sorry,' she said. 'I know it's awful for you—awful!'

Henrietta stepped back sharply from Julie's embrace. It occurred to her that Julie had dressed in a way that she thought suitable for the scene of a murder. Instead of her usual tight, short skirt, patterned stockings and high-heeled boots, she was wearing a plain dress of dark grey that reached almost to her ankles and flat-heeled black slippers. Her tawny curls were smoothed back from her forehead and tied at the back of her head with a black ribbon.

'It's awful for all of us,' Henrietta said stiffly.

'Yes, yes, of course, but I thought specially . . .' Julie paused. She looked round the room. 'Where's Patrick?'

'In London,' Henrietta said.

'Ah, how very—well, I was going to say convenient, but that doesn't sound quite right, does it?' Julie said. She turned to Brightmore. 'Well, Inspector, how can I help you?'

'I was given the impression you had certain things to tell us, Miss Bishop,' he answered. 'Isn't that what you said on the telephone?'

'Was it? Perhaps it was. I was in a state of shock. I don't really know what I said. I'm sure you can understand that.' She looked round for a chair and seeing her doing this, Charlie quickly swept some papers off one and offered it to her. She sank on to it gratefully. 'Yes, of course there's something I wanted to tell you. No, to ask you. Has anyone told you about Professor Franks's papers? All about things she'd been working on for some years. I believe after the fire she told people they'd gone up in smoke, but this isn't true. They're quite safe in the files in her office. I don't know if that means anything or not.'

'But you feel it's important to tell us this at just this moment,' Brightmore said. 'Can you explain that?'

'Well, it could have been just hysteria, couldn't it, saying they were lost?' Julie said. 'But it could mean she wanted to impress us with the fact that she'd have had nothing to gain by setting the house on fire herself. Those papers were very precious to her. She'd never have left them to burn. And she didn't, I can assure you of that, but she may have forgotten that I knew where she kept them, or may have assumed I wouldn't understand what they were. I'm no scientist and of course I didn't understand them, but I did know they were her life's work. I know how she cared about them.'

'So what you're telling us is that she may have had something to do with setting her house on fire, presumably to get the insurance, even though you're the person who gave her an alibi for the time the place was actually set alight,' Brightmore said. 'Is that what you're telling us?'

'I'm only telling you it's possible. She certainly didn't set it alight herself, but perhaps she got someone to do it for her.'

'Who would do such a thing?'

She did not answer, but looked round the room once more, her gaze coming to rest for a little longer on Henrietta's face than on that of anyone else.

Brightmore went on, 'Are you thinking of someone who was perhaps indebted to her in some way, so that he did it as a favour, or someone over whom she had power of some sort, or someone who perhaps hoped to share in the profit she'd make when she got the insurance?'

'How can I possibly tell?' For a moment she hid her face in her hands. Then suddenly looking round the room again, she exclaimed, 'Dr Robarts isn't here!'

'Why should he be?' Brightmore asked.

'Only that before I left home I phoned to tell him what had happened, and he said he'd come here straight away. I expect he'll be along any time now. But I thought Dr Carey would be here, and those two will have something to decide between them. You see, someone will have to take over the running of the department, just temporarily, you know, before they get round to appointing a new Professor, and it'll obviously be Dr Carey or Dr Robarts. I don't know who's responsible for arranging that sort of thing, the VC, or if it's a faculty matter or what, but I expect it will really be decided by those two.'

'And whoever does it is liable to become the next Professor, is that what you're telling me?'

'Certainly not,' Charlie Hedden said. 'The post will be advertised in the normal way and I should guess that someone from outside will almost certainly be brought in.'

'So there's a motive that sounded good to my uneducated understanding gone up in smoke,' Brightmore said with the irony that tended to creep into his voice. 'But there's a matter now on which I must question you, Miss Bishop. Did you leave the department before or after Professor Franks?'

'After her, I think,' Julie answered. 'I'm not sure.'

'Was it raining when you left?'

'It was just beginning.'

'Do you know how she left? I mean, did she leave in a friend's car, or by taxi, or did she walk?'

'I'm afraid I don't know. It might have been in Dr Robarts's car. He stayed fairly late this evening, so if she stayed late—but I don't think she did, I think she left fairly early.'

'Anyway, you didn't see her leave with anyone?'

'No—and here's Dr Robarts. Perhaps he can tell you something.'

The door had just been opened and Robarts had come into the room. He stood still just inside the door and looked round, till he met the gaze of Detective-Inspector Brightmore.

'Was I right to come?' Robarts asked. 'When Miss

Bishop phoned I felt it was what I ought to do, but if I'm
in the way I'll go home.'

'No, no, we're grateful you've come,' Brightmore said.
'And since you have, perhaps you can tell us something
about a matter we've just been discussing with Miss Bishop.
Do you know if you left the Department of Biochemistry
before or after Professor Franks this evening?'

'Oh, after,' Robarts answered without hesitation. 'I
stayed on fairly late, trying to make up for some time I
wasted this morning. Of course everything in the place is
at sixes and sevens. None of us know what we should be
doing. And now—now that this awful thing has happened
—God knows what we'll do.' His heavy, pale face looked
blankly bewildered.

'We were discussing that a few minutes ago,' Brightmore
said. 'Miss Bishop is of the opinion that one of you will
have to take charge temporarily, and that that will probably
mean Dr Carey or yourself.'

'Not me,' Robarts said quickly. 'I'm shortly leaving for
America and will have to get to work making my arrange-
ments for going. Where is Dr Carey, incidentally?'

'In London,' Henrietta replied.

'So we've been told,' Julie Bishop said with a little bite
in her voice. 'No doubt he'll be able to prove that when he
gets back. That brother of his, who he says he may have
gone to see, will probably supply him with an alibi, if the
time comes when he needs one.'

'Julie, you're a bitch!' Simon said explosively. 'Of course
he doesn't need one.'

The door opened again and Patrick walked in.

# Nine

His eyes met Henrietta's across the room. It had been her impulse to dart across to him and take him in her arms. She sat still.

'Seems I'm a bit late,' he remarked.

'It might have been useful if you'd been here earlier,' Brightmore said, 'but better late than never. Will you tell us what you've been doing?'

'Didn't my wife tell you?' Patrick said. 'I've been to London.'

'But she seems to have known no more than any of us why you went there.'

'Oh, I see. Well, I didn't have time to explain if I was going to catch the train. Besides, there was always a possibility that I was on a wild goose chase. And perhaps I was. Even now I'm not sure.'

'Have you seen David?' Henrietta asked. 'That's why you went to London, wasn't it? You'd somehow found out where you could get hold of him.'

'David?' Patrick said vaguely, as if the name meant nothing to him. 'Oh, David! No. I haven't seen him. Why, did you think perhaps I had?'

'I couldn't think of any other reason why you should rush off to London.'

'But why should I have wanted to see him? I mean, once it occurred to me that it probably wasn't Emma who was meant to die in the fire. I'm sure that's occurred to you by now, Inspector. But I'm sorry I went. I mean, once it struck me that there'd been one attempt on Margaret's life which hadn't come off, I ought to have realized there'd be another. I did, I suppose, only I didn't think it would come so soon.

Now I feel it's my fault. I could have prevented it, even if I'd no proof of anything.'

'You can prove that you went to London, I suppose,' Brightmore said. 'There's someone there you saw.'

'Oh yes,' Patrick said. 'A man called Evesham. Eric Evesham. He's Professor of Biochemistry at Wellford College. An old friend. A fellow student, actually. We spent most of the afternoon together.'

Someone in the room drew his breath in sharply. Henrietta was not sure who it was, but she was inclined to think that it was Simon Quinn. But Robarts was standing near him and the sound might have come from him. She saw Julie look quickly at the two men, as if she too had heard it, but Brightmore gave no sign of having heard anything. It would take more than a slight gasp, Henrietta thought, to make him show if he had suspicions of anyone in particular. Probably he was accustomed to hearing people gasping, groaning, crying, even screaming, without assuming that it was evidence of guilt.

'Are you going to tell us what took you to see Professor Evesham?' Brightmore asked. 'I have to tell you that you are not obliged to do so.'

'Oh, I realize that,' Patrick said, 'and the matter's complicated. And before I go on with it, there's something I'd like to ask you. Has anyone here been into my lab this afternoon? Or did anyone see anyone else go in? What about you, Julie?'

She shook her head. 'I didn't go in.'

'But did you see anyone else go in?'

'Well, let me think. No. Yes, I did. My door was open and I saw Dr Robarts pass and go into your lab about half past three. Then he asked me if I knew where you were and I said if you weren't in your lab you might have gone home.'

'You thought he was looking for me, did you?'

'Yes, of course.'

Patrick looked at Robarts. 'Is that correct?'

Robarts nodded without answering.

'So you saw him go in and come out, did you, Julie?'
Patrick asked.

'That's right,' she said.

'Did you happen to notice if he was carrying anything,
or perhaps had something a bit heavy in a pocket?'

'He was carrying a briefcase, but that's all I remember.'
She turned to Robarts. 'That was all, wasn't it? You were
carrying a briefcase, weren't you?'

'Certainly,' Robarts said, his heavy, pale face hardening
with anger. 'Inspector, do you intend to let this inquisition
go on? You've made it clear we haven't got to answer your
questions, but is there any reason why we should be subject
to the sort of inquiry Dr Carey is taking it on himself to
make without having explained why he's asking such
questions?'

'I was wondering when one of you was going to ask
that,' Brightmore observed with his wry little smile. 'Very
interesting, watching someone trying to get the information
you'd like to get yourself when he's what you might call an
amateur, but happens to have connections with everyone
involved in the case. And of course, with the case itself,
there are all kinds of rules about police procedure to prevent
you going at it hard-headed yourself. Have you any more
questions you'd like to ask, Dr Carey? If you have, I'd like
to hear what they are.'

'I'd just like to ask Miss Bishop if she saw Mr Quinn go
into my lab,' Patrick replied. 'Did you, Julie?'

'No,' she said, 'but I didn't leave my door open all the
afternoon. Anyone might have gone in.'

'Yes, of course,' Patrick said. 'Well, Simon, did you go
in?'

'No,' Simon grunted.

'And you don't know of anyone who did—some student,
even, who might have been looking for me?'

'No.'

'Because, you see, something's missing from my lab. I went in for a few minutes on my way home from the station, actually looking for Professor Franks, and when I didn't find her in her room, I took a quick look in my own room at an experiment I've got going, and straightaway I noticed something that's normally there but wasn't then. A pestle. That's a funny sort of thing to have disappeared, isn't it?'

'A pestle?' Brightmore said questioningly, showing that he had not understood.

'Yes, you know—a mortar and pestle. Things you use for grinding things up. Well, the mortar's there, but the pestle isn't.'

A sudden look of interest appeared on the Inspector's face.

'Would you describe this pestle to me, please?'

'Well, it's made of glass. Frosted glass. And I suppose it's about seven or eight inches long and it's solid.'

'Pretty heavy, then?'

'Oh yes, quite heavy.'

'But it could disappear into a pocket, a fairly large pocket?'

'I think so.'

'Or perhaps a briefcase.'

'Inspector!' Robarts suddenly shouted furiously. 'Are you and Carey cooking up the idea that this pestle was the blunt instrument that was used to kill Professor Franks, and that it was taken from Carey's lab in my briefcase?'

The Inspector and Patrick exchanged glances, then the Inspector shook his head.

'I don't know what Dr Carey may have in his mind, but before I leap to any conclusion whatever, I shall conduct a fairly thorough search, not only of this house, but its garden, and the gardens near it. I find the idea that this pestle might be the blunt instrument, as you call it, that killed Professor Franks distinctly interesting. But as to whether it is, and whether it may be concealed somewhere here, I'm naturally keeping an entirely open mind. Wild guesses aren't much in my line—Yes?' he said, breaking off what he had been saying and looking towards the door at which the constable who had come in before had reappeared.

'The photographers have finished,' he said, 'and the ambulance people want to know if they can remove the body.'

Brightmore stood up.

'Probably,' he said. 'I'm just coming.' He looked round the room. 'Will you all be staying here? You're at liberty to go home if you want to.'

'Can my wife and I go up to our flat?' Patrick said.

'Certainly.'

'And can I go up to mine?' Simon asked quickly. 'My poor wife's probably going out of her mind with worry by now, but she couldn't leave Tessa.'

'Yes, I'll know where to find you later if you should be wanted.'

'I'd like to go home,' Julie said. 'I live with my parents and I always cook the supper for them.'

'And I thought you'd stay and have a bite of supper with me,' Charlie Hedden said. 'What about it?'

She hesitated. 'Well, if it wouldn't be any trouble, Dr Hedden . . . But I'd have to phone them at home and tell them why I wasn't coming back.'

He waved towards the telephone. 'Go ahead.'

But before she had moved towards it, Robarts said harshly, 'I'm going home.'

Without paying any attention to this discussion, Inspector Brightmore and Sergeant Dance left the room. Patrick looked at Henrietta and she went to his side. But before they could leave, Simon Quinn darted swiftly past them and in his usual way went racing up the stairs. Henrietta and Patrick followed him more slowly.

The gas fire had been alight in their sitting-room ever since Charlie had fetched her from it so wildly, and it was very warm. She went to the fire and turned it down. Then she went to the window and put her face close to the glass, gazing out into the darkness.

'I think the rain's stopped,' she said.

Patrick went up to her and put his arms around her.

'I'm sorry I wasn't here when it all happened,' he said.

She turned in his arms and kissed him. Then she stepped away from him and drew the curtains.

'And what did David have to say to you?' she asked.

'David?' he said, as if the question took him by surprise, then he laughed. It seemed strange to hear even that brief laugh after what they had been through downstairs. 'Oh yes, David. That he's going to get married, as a matter of fact. How did you know I'd seen him?'

'Something about the tone of your voice downstairs when you spoke about him. Are you serious? Is he getting married?'

'It's possible. One of the awful things about confirmed liars is that they sometimes tell the truth.'

'But you did see him?'

'Yes, I did. I was going to tell you what I meant to do, but when I got home this morning you were out, and I was just trying to make up my mind what to do when David rang up. He asked if there was any chance of my coming to London sometime soon, because he wanted to talk to me, so I told him I'd be up today and we arranged that he should meet me at Euston. And I thought, of course, that what he wanted to talk about was the fire here and the death of Emma, and I began to wonder if he'd really been more involved in it than I'd thought. We met and had lunch in the cafeteria at the station, and it turned out that what he wanted was to tell me he was getting married to a Lady Helena Deedham, an earl's daughter, and he was particularly anxious I shouldn't let her know anything about his marriage to Emma. He was sure, you see, that the marriage would get into the illustrated papers and I'd see it and feel I ought to tell her something about his past, because she thinks he's an explorer who's been spending the last few years of his life in darkest Africa. Knowing Kenya very well and a bit about Uganda and so on had helped him to build up his image and she was fascinated by it, and the two of them were intending to run a pub together. They'd got their eye on one in Dorset. I suppose it might work. She, of course, is supplying the money and by now, with all his wandering, he's got a fair amount of know-how. I told him, of course, I didn't read the kind of papers he was worrying about, and shouldn't have seen anything about it.'

'Didn't he try to get any money out of you?' Henrietta asked.

'Oh yes, naturally.' Patrick looked a little guilty. 'As a matter of fact, I let him have most of what I had on me, which was only about a hundred pounds, and he was rather disgusted with it, but seemed to think it was better than nothing.'

'But you didn't promise him any more?'

'Oh no.'

'Thank goodness. But do the daughters of earls really run pubs nowadays?'

'I don't see why they shouldn't, any more than anyone else, if they're that way inclined, though I hope they won't take to pushing drugs.'

'And did you believe a word of it?'

He laughed. 'It's so unlikely, it might be true. Now, what about a drink?'

'All right. But I still want to know what really took you to London. Why did you want to see Eric?'

'To ask him if he knew of any jobs that were likely to be going anywhere in the immediate future. He's got his ear to the ground about things like that. And to ask him if he thought there'd be any point in my getting in touch with anyone in the research councils. Because, my dear, I think we've got to leave Knotlington. Don't you agree? You see, I'm almost certain I know who murdered both Margaret and Emma, but if it can't be proved I couldn't face going on working with him. It's partly that I couldn't face meeting him day after day, and partly that I'd keep wondering when he'd think it was best for him to clobber me. Now let's have that drink, then I'll tell you all about it.'

He went to fetch the whisky and glasses and they sat down on either side of the gas fire and Henrietta waited for Patrick to go on. But even after some minutes he seemed reluctant to do it. He stared into his glass and frowned and looked as if he felt that he had already said too much, then he looked up at her with an apologetic smile, as if he knew that he had no right to keep her waiting, but felt an intense unwillingness to say any more.

She tried to help him. 'You know Robarts isn't staying here? He's going to Berkeley.'

'That's fixed up, is it?' he said.

'I believe so. So you wouldn't be meeting him day after day, would you?'

'No.'

'So he isn't the person you suspect.'

'No.'

'It's Simon, isn't it?'

He drew a deep breath, nodded and said, 'Yes.'

'And you don't know what to do about it, because of Rachel and Tessa.'

He gave a melancholy nod. 'But what's put you on to him?'

'Oh, this and that. Your saying just now that you wouldn't be able to face meeting him day after day, when I knew you couldn't mean Robarts. And his arriving late at our party and standing still suddenly the moment he came into the room and saw Margaret bright and alive when he imagined he'd killed her. Not that that meant anything to me until I realized that the word was going about that it was Margaret who was meant to have been killed in the fire, and not Emma. Simon couldn't have had any possible motive for turning the key on Emma that locked her into the burning house.'

'No, but what was his motive for killing Margaret?'

'I haven't the slightest idea.'

'Nor had I until I remembered the business of the Ph.D.'

'I don't understand. Didn't Margaret want him to work for a Ph.D.? That would have led to promotion for him, wouldn't it?'

'But he refused to try for it.'

'Didn't that mean that he was just too lazy?'

'He isn't lazy, you know. He works very hard and he's fairly competent. But he'd have had to register for it, and give some references, for instance, the head of the department in which he'd taken his degree. And his refusal to do that started Margaret thinking. That much I know for certain, because I checked it today with Eric Evesham. Simon always said he'd been at Wellford, and if he had been, even if it had been before Eric's time, it would have been easy for Eric to find out if what Simon said about himself was true. And Margaret got on to him some weeks ago, so Eric told me, and asked him what he could tell her about Simon. And all Eric could tell her was that Simon had never been to Wellford at all. He hadn't got a degree, and was probably a complete fraud. And once she knew that, it put him in her power, you see. She could easily have had him sacked, if she'd wanted to, and cut off from doing any serious scientific work anywhere else, however much he wanted to. Or she could use him to do what she happened to want done. And we know what that was. She wanted her house burnt down.'

Henrietta sipped her whisky and thought about it.

'And it was just his refusing to work for a Ph.D. that put you on to it, was it?' she asked.

'Oh, there've been other odds and ends as well. I noticed, though I didn't think much about it, that he'd never talk about Wellford. I know a number of the people working there, but if I ever asked him anything about them, what he thought of their work or how he'd got on with them, he'd always avoid giving any sort of answer and change the subject. I didn't think anything much about it at the time. I thought the fact probably was that he'd been unhappy there and didn't like to talk about it. But then yesterday I suddenly thought the truth might be that he'd never been there at all. I began to think about how very little I really knew about him. When I persuaded Margaret to take him on here I really knew very little. I'd met him at the odd conference and talked to him a good deal and been impressed by his ability. But I'd taken his word for what he had in the way of formal qualifications, and the fact that the grant on which he'd been living for the last couple of years was soon coming to an end and he couldn't get a job. My belief is now that he'd been a technician in one of the research councils' laboratories, and could have kept his job there for as long as he liked, but he was desperate to get working in pure science. If I'm right about all this, it's a very tragic story really, because he could easily have got a degree if he'd started off in the right way. If he'd ever been honest with me about it all before I got him the appointment here, I could probably have fixed things so that he could work for a degree. But I rather think he's one of the people like my dear brother David who actually prefers doing things dishonestly. It gives him a pleasing feeling of having put one over on other people and made it possible for him to despise them.'

'Did you think of his having been late for our party and the shock he seemed to have when he came into the room?' Henrietta asked.

'Only when I'd found out the fraud about his qualifications, because it was only then I realized how much he was
in Margaret's power.'

'And you really believe she got him to burn her house
down? And got herself an alibi by getting Julie to bring her
to our party?'

'Well, didn't we think it was an oddly uncharacteristic
thing for her to do? She doesn't go to parties. We didn't
expect her to come. But probably she'd told Simon, when
she arranged with him to go to the house and gave him the
key to it, that she'd really go to the party and that that was
when he could do the job for her. And he went there to do
it, and suddenly through the window he believed he saw
her. He thought she hadn't gone to the party after all, and
realized he'd only got to turn the key of the room on her
before setting things alight to be free of her. Only it was
the wrong woman who was burnt to death.'

'And Margaret knew just what he'd done.'

'Of course. But you see, she was almost as much in his
power now as he was in hers. If she let on to the police, or
to anyone, that she knew he'd killed Emma, she'd have to
admit that she herself had arranged for arson to defraud
the insurance people. And the only thing for her and Simon
to do was to call it quits and say nothing about one another,
and I think that was why she came up here this evening,
to have a quiet talk with him and arrange that they'd both
say nothing about the whole matter. Only she didn't realize
the kind of man he was, or that he'd got a heavy glass
pestle in his pocket.'

'And what are we going to do about it? Keep quiet too?'

'That's the question. What shall we do?'

'Because of Rachel and Tessa?'

He got up and started to roam about the room. 'Yes,' he
said, 'because of Rachel and Tessa.'

'How much of this do you think she perhaps knows?'

'I don't know. You know her better than I do. Would

Simon have told her what had happened, or would she have guessed it?'

'I only know that on Saturday morning she told me that now she'd got Tessa she was almost perfectly happy.'

'She really said that?'

'Yes.'

'D'you know, I find it curiously unconvincing. People only say that kind of thing when they're trying to convince themselves.'

'So you think she'd begun to understand the kind of person he was, but didn't want to admit it to herself.'

'Isn't it possible?'

'All the same, what are we going to do about her?'

'Oh, we needn't do anything. There isn't a shred of proof of all the things I've been saying to you. We can stay quiet and leave the police to arrive at what conclusion they like. Then we shouldn't have the responsibility of ruining Rachel's life for her.'

'Simon was prepared to try to ruin our lives. He planted Margaret's key on us. He was trying to frame you.'

Patrick's face was sad. 'I've known for quite a while he doesn't like me. As long as we only met casually it was fine, but when I became virtually his boss, it was fatal. Simon's someone who's got to hate his boss, whoever he is and however much he's done for him. I could see it developing, and couldn't think of what I ought to do. It worried me a good deal, because I was quite fond of the little bastard.'

'You never said anything about it.'

'No, why should I?'

'We've nearly always shared our worries. About David, for instance.'

'Well, I'd have told you everything in the end. And you seemed to have a good relationship with Rachel, and I didn't want to spoil that.'

'But what ought we to do now, Patrick? Go upstairs and confront the two of them with all these things you've been telling me and let her get the blow full in the face, or tell the police, and let them do it if they want to, or do nothing and see if she can go on being perfectly happy with a man who's twice committed murder?'

'Isn't it tempting to do just that?'

'Except that she might even not be safe. If he knew at some time that he'd somehow betrayed himself to her, mightn't he find some quick and easy way of getting rid of her?'

He stopped his roaming and stood still, turning on her a face that had suddenly become deeply anxious and haggard. He had the look of someone who was imploring to be let off some task that was too much for him, too difficult, too painful.

At that moment the doorbell rang.

Patrick did not move, so Henrietta got up and went out to the hall to answer the bell. When she opened the door she found Rachel facing her. She had something in her hand which she held out to Henrietta. She did not immediately recognize what it was, then realized that it was an object made of frosted glass and was about seven or eight inches long. In fact, the pestle missing from Patrick's laboratory.

'Rachel, Rachel, think what you're doing,' she begged.

'I know what I'm doing,' Rachel answered in a strange voice of extreme detachment. There was an emptiness about her eyes, as if she were in a state of shock.

'Come in, then,' Henrietta said.

'No, I must go back to Tessa,' the remote voice said. 'He's gone, you know, though I don't suppose he'll get far. But he left this behind, and I can't bear having it in the flat, so will you please take it? You needn't be afraid of smudging fingerprints. I washed them off it, and the blood too, of course. And you mustn't worry about me, because a wife can't give evidence against her husband and if the police come to question me I shall tell them I know that and just say nothing else at all. I won't be involved.'

Patrick had joined Henrietta in the doorway.

'But how did you find out what had happened, Rachel?' he asked.

'First of all because of the petrol he bought in cans when we didn't need any, and then because of his sitting up crying all night because he'd killed an innocent person. I think finding he'd done that made him a little mad. He said he'd got to pay the Professor out for what she'd made him do, that it was all her fault because she was a wicked woman and tonight he told me how he'd done it. But I won't go into all that. I just want you to take care of the pestle. Now I really must go back to Tessa. I'm not sure I haven't gone a little mad myself, but perhaps that will pass. Madness is infectious. Did you know that? A lot of people don't know it, but it's a scientific fact. Good night.'

She turned and ran quickly up the stairs to the flat above.

# Ten

Rachel had been right. Simon did not get very far. He got as far as the garage, where he was just unlocking the door of his car when two constables saw him and wanted to know where he was going. Even then, if he had kept his head, he might have been able to get as far as the University, though a police car would have followed him, as one had unobtrusively followed Neil Robarts, and in that large and complicated building Simon might have been able to melt into its intricacy and disappear. But as soon as one of the men touched him on the shoulder and began to ask his question about Simon's intentions, he began to shout, 'She'll tell you everything! She'll tell you everything!' The shouting then rose to incomprehensible screaming, which went on as the two big men led the small and strangely wilting Simon to their own car and drove him to the police station.

There he could not even be persuaded to wait a little while before he poured out his confession. Not that he said much about his attack on Margaret Franks. It was about having been responsible for the burning alive of Emma Carey that he had to tell as many people as possible. He blamed Margaret Franks for it, almost as if she had done it herself, or at least had forced him to do it, and so she herself had deserved to die. That she had done so seemed to strike him as a minor matter. Detective-Inspector Brightmore, who listened to him, as the flood of information poured out, did not look at all pleased with it. Simon could merely be preparing a defence of diminished responsibility. He was certainly behaving as if he was quite out of his mind, which possibly he really was, but it had to be remembered that he was a clever little man who had deceived people who Inspector Brightmore was modestly convinced were far cleverer than he was himself and it might be what he was bent on achieving now.

During the evening Patrick telephoned the police station to tell the Inspector that he was in possession of the pestle which he had stated had vanished from his laboratory. But it was not on that evidence, or over his theory of the crimes that Patrick later explained to the Inspector, that Simon was convicted. Witnesses were discovered who had seen Professor Franks leaving the University on the Monday evening in Simon Quinn's car. One, a student, was even found who had seen Simon go into Patrick's laboratory and seen him come out clutching something in a pocket which was obviously heavy. A young couple who had been making use of the quiet lane behind Margaret Franks's house for their own purposes just before it burst into flames, had seen a small man, whom they both identified as Simon, come out of the door that opened on to the lane from her back yard. He was sentenced to life imprisonment, though the lawyer continued to argue whether it should not have been a case of his being detained at Her Majesty's pleasure.

Rachel, with Tessa, left Knotlington immediately after the two inquests to stay with her married sister who lived in Yorkshire. Simon had been mistaken, she told no one anything of what she knew. While she was still in the flat above the Careys', Henrietta made two or three attempts to see her, to offer what comfort she could, but she was met with a blank face with stony, expressionless eyes, and the voice that answered her always had an eerie note of detachment, as if Rachel were speaking to someone who was not actually there. Henrietta was never invited into the flat, but one day she heard the footsteps of several people overhead, and she later had a talk with a grave, kind-faced young woman who explained that she was Rachel's sister from Yorkshire and was in Knotlington for the time being with her husband, and that on the whole she believed that what Rachel needed most for the time being was to be left alone. With some relief Henrietta gave up her attempt to be a good Samaritan.

She and Patrick had problems of their own just then. He had been asked by the Vice Chancellor to take over the running of the Department of Biochemistry until a new head was appointed. This had happened after Robarts had made it clear that he could not undertake this work because he was shortly leaving for Berkeley. Meanwhile, Patrick had heard of an appointment in a London college which it seemed he had a very good chance of obtaining. If he had been ready to stay in Knotlington he would probably have been offered the vacant Chair, but he could not bring himself to step into the dead woman's shoes. A woman who had managed to be both friend and enemy at the same time, a strange achievement.

Malcolm Mackintosh retired at the end of the summer term and he and his wife were given the excellent dinner that they had expected, and to which the members of the department where he had worked for so many years all came, and also students who had worked under him, many of them now middle-aged and in more responsible posts than he. A complete set of stainless steel cutlery, chosen by his wife Marie, was presented to the Mackintoshes; then they set off on what they had been promising themselves for a long time, a trip round the world. Henrietta and Patrick went to the airport to see them off on their first hop to Heathrow, after which they would be making for Mexico City. In the end they did not settle in a cottage in the Highlands, but in one in a village in Somerset.

Julie Bishop remained in Knotlington, assuming that she would retain her appointment as secretary to the new professor, when one could be found. She once said something to Patrick, over an unusual drink in the Staff Club, which he took to be an admission that it had been she who had sent the anonymous card to Emma Carey, giving her

Patrick's correct title and address, but as soon as he tried
to persuade her to state this clearly, she claimed that he
had entirely misunderstood her and that of course it had
been Professor Franks who had written. From that time,
however, he was certain that it was Julie who had done so,
which meant that indirectly she was responsible for two
deaths.

But someone else had even more responsibility than she
and that was David Carey, of whom Patrick and Henrietta
heard nothing more after his meeting with Patrick at Euston
until a brief letter arrived not from Dorset but from Bar-
bados, saying that he had just opened a small hotel and
would make them very welcome if they should feel inclined
to spend a holiday on the island. He added at the end of
the letter that he was very happily married.

Some months later Henrietta again visited her mother
and told her in detail all that had happened since she had
last been with her. She told her about David's letter and
showed her a photograph that had been enclosed with it.
It was a wedding photograph and showed David in a pale
grey suit, tanned and smiling and looking remarkably handsome. The woman at his side was in a white wedding-dress,
with a wreath of flowers on her crisply curling dark hair
and a beaming smile on her face, showing splendid white
teeth. She seemed to be nearly as tall as he was, with broad
shoulders, a full bosom, a round, plumply charming face
and glittering dark eyes. There was a look of strength and
good nature about her. She was also quite black.

'Do you think she looks like Lady Helena Deedham?'
Henrietta asked. 'David didn't actually mention her name.'

'I think either Lady Henrietta or he himself may have
had second thoughts about that marriage.' Mrs Lanchester
handed the photograph back to Henrietta and picked up
the knitting again on which she was working. It was a
cardigan for Patrick, for she was convinced that the last
one she had knitted for him several years ago and to which

he was too devoted to discard it, must in fact be in holes by now. 'He seems to be a very marrying man, doesn't he? One wonders why he bothers about it nowadays.;

'I suppose it gives him a sense of security,' Henrietta said. 'It's something he's needed all his life.'

'For all we know, of course,' Mrs Lanchester said, 'he did marry Lady Helena, and is married to her still. Bigamy wouldn't seem much of an offence to him, compared with all the rest that he's got on his conscience.'

'You really think he was to blame for all that happened in Knotlington?'

'Not for Professor Franks's house being set on fire, of course,' her mother said. 'That crime was her own doing. But if he hadn't married that poor girl in Aberdeen in Patrick's name, she'd never have come to Knotlington looking for him. And then she wouldn't have gone looking for Professor Franks to tell her that Patrick hadn't actually married her and wasn't a bigamist, and Simon Quinn wouldn't have mistaken her for the Professor and locked her into the room she was in where she was burnt to death. And then he wouldn't have gone crazy at having killed an innocent woman and killed Professor Franks in revenge for what he considered she'd made him do. Of course other people were to blame as well, but it all began with David, didn't it, though he never laid a finger on anyone?'

'I wonder how much this woman he's married knows about him,' Henrietta said.

'It wouldn't surprise me at all if she understands perfectly well what she's taken on,' Mrs Lanchester replied. 'But she'll be quite capable of keeping him in order, making him work for his living in this hotel he says they've opened. I suppose she had the money with which they started it. And if he tells her lies she'll just laugh at him which will be very good for him. I've a feeling, you know, that marrying her is the one sensible thing he's ever done in his life, and I think you and Patrick might really consider accepting his invitation and go and visit them.'

'You think the hotel really exists there?' Henrietta said.

'Ah, of course,' Mrs Lanchester said, frowning as she concentrated on the pattern that she was knitting, 'that's quite a question.'